LEGACY OF REGRET

When Liz Shepherd unexpectedly inherits an elderly man's considerable estate, she is persuaded it is in gratitude for her kindness to him. But doubts set in when Steve Lewis, in the guise of a reporter, challenges her good luck. Was there another reason for her legacy? And why is Steve so interested? She comes to regret her inheritance and all its uncertainties — until Steve helps her find the truth and they discover the secret of their past.

Books by Jo James
in the Linford Romance Library:

CHANCE ENCOUNTER
THE RELUCTANT BACHELOR
SHADOWS ACROSS THE WATER
SECRET OF THE RIDGE
AN UNEASY ARRANGEMENT
MYSTERY AT BLUFF COTTAGE
IMPETUOUS HEART
TOO MANY YESTERDAYS
TAKING A CHANCE
HOUSE OF SECRETS
SOPHIE'S FOLLY
A FAMILY SECRET
CHASING SHADOWS

JO JAMES

◆

LEGACY OF REGRET

Complete and Unabridged

LINFORD
Leicester

First published in Great Britain in 2007

First Linford Edition
published 2008

British Library CIP Data

James, Jo
    Legacy of regret.—Large print ed.—
Linford romance library
    1. Inheritance and succession—Fiction
    2. Family secrets—Fiction 3. Love stories
    4. Large type books
    I. Title
    823.9'2 [F]

    ISBN 978–1–84782–106–5

Published by
F. A. Thorpe (Publishing)
Anstey, Leicestershire

Set by Words & Graphics Ltd.
Anstey, Leicestershire
Printed and bound in Great Britain by
T. J. International Ltd., Padstow, Cornwall

This book is printed on acid-free paper

1

Liz Shepherd was still in a daze when she came down in the lift clasping the notes she'd written at the meeting. Back on the street, she tucked them into her shoulder bag and glanced at her wristwatch. Time to get back to *Fantastic Flowers*, the hospital-based florist shop where she worked, but she still felt giddy with excitement.

As she walked along Melbourne's legal precinct her feet hardly touched the pavement, and anxious to mull over what had happened at the interview, she hurried into the first coffee shop she came to. There, she ordered cappuccino and as an afterthought added a chocolate muffin. Why not? She had something to celebrate; something she still had to pinch herself to believe was true.

Tonight, she'd go through her notes

again, make sure she hadn't dreamt it all. Breaking the muffin with her fingers, she popped a portion into her mouth, but she couldn't wait. She wiped her slightly sticky fingers with a serviette, retrieved her notes from her bag and began studying them.

Thank goodness they still said the same thing. Thank goodness the interview she'd just had did actually take place. It was so mind blowing, so out of left field she might risk ringing Hayden at work. Mr Bowlen junior had asked her not to talk about her good fortune for the present, but telling her boyfriend, who was a company lawyer, would be all right.

Another bite into her muffin and she dismissed the idea, remembering his constant rebukes. 'Elizabeth, you know I can't talk now. I'm in conference.' And if he wasn't in conferences, he was about to go into court.

For all his success and good looks, Hayden could sometimes be a bit pompous. She and her flatmate, Angie, often had a bit of a laugh about it. Hey, why not phone Angie? She took out her mobile, but on second thoughts, she decided against that call, too. They could get involved in a long conversation and she was due back at the shop fifteen minutes ago.

Her boss, Melba, came across to her later as she was about to knock off and tapped her on the shoulder. 'Liz, you've created some beautiful presentation arrangements this afternoon. When you took the hour off, I thought it may have been bad news, but clearly something's inspired you?'

Liz smiled, but after Mr Bowlen's caution decided not to confide in her boss for the moment. 'The autumn roses are an inspiration in themselves.'

Going home, she travelled fifteen minutes by tram from the hospital, and alighting, took a short walk to the apartment she shared with Angie. She paused, as usual, outside *Wellington Grange*, the once stately residence on the main street with its white render, its

3

genuine lacework across the ground and upper storey verandahs, the long casement windows, the decorative leadlight, and once beautifully-landscaped gardens.

After old Tom Lawson moved in it had slowly started to lose some of its sheen, and since his death a few weeks ago, it had taken on a lonely, abandoned appearance. Now her heart skipped several beats, as she opened the gate uncertainly and strolled around the garden. How wonderful it would be to restore it to its former beauty she thought, unsure why Tom hadn't done that.

She'd become friendly with him soon after she moved in for she often found him strolling in the garden when she passed by. They'd chatted, mainly about flowers, and she willingly spent time with him for he was obviously lonely, hungry for someone to talk to.

She shrugged, reluctantly closed the gate behind her and moved on quickening her step, hoping Angie would already be home. On a rush of adrenaline she took the stairs to the first floor of the block of apartments two at a time, anxious to share her news with her best friend.

Happily she found the door already unlocked, and pushed it ajar, calling, 'Get out the champagne, Angie, we've got something to celebrate.'

Angie was filling the kettle. She turned, grinning. 'I can tell from your expression and your voice, you're not in any trouble with the law, and thank goodness for that, but whatever your news, it hardly calls for champagne — tea will have to do. What was Bowlen and Bowlen's summons to their law firm all about?'

'I'm not supposed to tell anyone for now, and frankly I'm taking a risk telling someone as spontaneous as you, but I'm so excited, I have to share it.'

'Will you get on with it, Liz.'

'You remember Tom Lawson?'

'The old bloke up the road — the

one you kind of adopted like a stray kitten?'

Liz smiled. 'I enjoyed talking to him. It was mostly about flowers and gardens and recipes. I always found him interesting — he was a real sweetie.'

'Whatever, I don't know how you stayed so patient. As I recall, you hardly ever got by that house without him bailing you up for a chinwag.'

Liz nodded, her mood swung slightly melancholic. 'Not any more, poor old darling. I actually miss him. I'm sure he'd had a tragedy in his life. He didn't seem to have a relative or a friend in the world, and really, I didn't mind spending time with him.'

The smile returned to Liz's eyes. She placed her notes on the table. 'Wait for it.' And doing a little jig, she announced. 'Old Tom has left me his estate.' The smile spread its rays to every corner of her face. 'Can you believe it? That beautiful old house — No. 4 *Wellington Grange* — is apparently mine along with Tom's considerable bank balance.'

As she gestured with her hands, she sent her mug crashing to the floor, the last of the tea puddled at her feet, but they both ignored it. 'The Junior Bowlen part — Michael — of the practice told me I've inherited everything.'

Angie's eyes widened. 'Fair dinkum?'

Liz nodded. 'Fair dinkum. It still seems unreal, but now I've actually said it, it gives the news some credibility. *Wellington Grange* will be mine once the legals have been finalised.'

Angie stepped over the tea puddle and hugged her energetically. 'Congratulations, Liz,' she said, adding with a wide grin, 'I know how to choose my friends, don't I? Now is there anything I can do for you, oh lady heiress?'

Liz smiled, shook her head. 'Can this really be happening?'

'Of course it's happening, Mr Bowlen Junior told you, didn't he? And men with names like Mr Bowlen Junior don't lie, not officially anyway.'

'Here, confirm it for me,' Liz said, grinning like a Cheshire cat as she pushed the notes she'd taken at the legal practice into her friend's hand.

Scanning them, Angie whooped, 'No doubt about it — overnight you've become a capitalist, a person of property as they say in the classics.' Turning serious, she added, 'It's remarkable.'

Liz felt a vague uneasiness.

'It is. I can't work it out. He hardly knew me, and to be honest I didn't think he owned the house or was wealthy. It doesn't really make a lot of sense.'

Angie shrugged. 'You probably don't realise how much your thoughtfulness meant to him. After he had his first heart attack, didn't you pop up to his hospital bed every day and take him little treats?'

'I was on the premises, it was nothing.'

'I seem to remember you making soup and pastries for him when he came home and organising people from home help and meals-on-wheels to call on him regularly. I think you're a real treasure, Liz. That's obviously what Tom thought, too.'

She tossed it off with, 'I did what any decent human being would, but I can't help wondering about his early life. Surely there were children, nephews, nieces, good friends he could have left it to.'

'If he had a family they clearly didn't care about him.'

Liz chewed on her bottom lip. 'We don't know, but supposing he did, even if he's fallen out with them, they'll be furious once they hear what he's done. And I won't be too popular with them either. Now that I've got over the shock and the excitement, I'm starting to feel uneasy. It's odd.'

'Stop worrying. He was of sound mind, your notes say, when he made his will. Think back, can you remember him ever talking about a family, ever seeing any of them call around? He may have been a bachelor.'

'Actually, I remember seeing a family photo in the lounge room.'

'His parents and brothers or sisters?'

Liz nodded, 'Could be, but I thought more likely his wife and children. It wasn't one of those old black and white photos. I asked him about it and he went the colour of beetroot. He told me it was his brother's family, and said he hadn't heard from them in years. Apparently he went to England on a business venture and made his money there, but he said it was the worst thing he ever did. He lost touch with his family.'

Angie began mopping up the tea from the floor with a cloth. 'There's your answer. He fell out with his family. So what did Hayden say? Are you two going out tonight to celebrate?'

Liz flopped on to a kitchen chair. 'Oh my gosh, I haven't told him yet.'

Walking across to the sink, Angie said, 'Sometimes I wonder about you. I'd have been on the phone to him the minute I heard.'

'You know he hates me phoning him at work.'

'Liz, you don't understand the man. This is news he's going to want to hear no matter how important the meeting he's in. If marriage is what you want, this makes it possible right now. You can move into *Wellington Grange* and live the grand life. I can imagine Hayden telling everyone he owns a beautiful home at the smart end of Parkville.' Angie lifted the handset and handed it to her. 'Phone him.'

Liz had been going out with Hayden for six months. He was what her mother, if she were alive, would have called 'a good catch'. Tallish, decisive, impeccable business clothes and manners, styled dark hair and hazel eyes that often flashed with impatience.

She started listening to her mother's advice after Mark Moody left her bruised and out of love with romance. He was gorgeous, relaxed, unreliable, unambitious, openly bragged surfing was his first love. And she thought her life was complete, until he did the ultimate romantic act and sailed off to the Bahamas in a yacht with an exotic dancer.

With Hayden, she congratulated herself on finding a man who was good-looking and offered security. He told her she was stunningly attractive and how much he enjoyed showing her off to his colleagues.

She placed the phone on the bench, frowned. 'Angie, Hayden hasn't talked marriage yet.'

'But he will, he will, especially now.'

Liz shrugged. 'You think my inheritance will prompt him to pop the question?'

'I don't think it, I'm predicting it.'

After receiving the news of her good fortune she found it difficult to focus for long on anything else. Now, a tight feeling knotted her stomach.

'Why should inheriting Tom Lawson's estate change anything between me and Hayden? I have no intention of rushing into marriage. My parents' relationship and the Mark Moody fiasco have made me extra cautious. I won't marry until I'm sure I've found the right man. It was painful watching my father turn into a moody, unhappy man who became dependent on alcohol. Besides, I think you're wrong about Hayden. It's not something he'll want to rush into either.'

'OK, OK,' Angie said, replacing the handset, grinning. 'I was checking to see if there's any hope for me with the eligible and handsome Hayden. So when are you going to tell him — about the estate I mean?'

Liz glanced fondly at her flatmate. She was so good natured with an impetuosity that sometimes landed them in awkward, but funny situations and the coolness to escape them, damage-free. Liz would miss her terribly if she gave up the flat.

'It hasn't occurred to me until now, but you'd be good for the man — straighten out some of the stuffy creases in his personality.' She paused, smiled. 'But Angie, he's not available.'

'Rats! You do remember I saw him first?'

'How can I forget?' Liz said with an amused tilt of her head, 'You got talking to him in the hospital while you waited for me to close the shop.'

'He took one look at you, one glance into those dazzling green eyes, and I was history. What on earth made me hook up with a woman who's much better looking and smarter than me? It's so deflating.'

Liz almost doubled over with laughter. 'Angie, you're gorgeous. The man lucky enough to get you will go through life forever sporting a turned up mouth and laughter lines.'

Angie raised dark brows. 'So if I've got so much going for me, why aren't the blokes queuing up? Which reminds me, if you don't ring Hayden to tell him about this momentous day, why don't we go out to celebrate in style?'

'What a super idea,' Liz said.

And as if the man knew they'd postponed speaking to him, the phone rang.

'Elizabeth, would you care to meet me for dinner tonight?' Hayden asked. 'I thought *Forbidden Fruit*. It's been highly recommended as a classy, intimate little restaurant.'

Liz disliked herself for feeling slightly annoyed. *Forbidden Fruit* was a yuppie restaurant, and she suspected that if she were to agree they'd 'accidentally' bump into several of his legal mates there. The conversation would inevitably centre on the latest judicial appointments and the share market gains. She wasn't in the mood. She was in celebration mood.

'I'm sorry, Hayden, but Angie and I are having a girls' night out.'

'But you can cancel surely,' he insisted, 'you can see Angie any time. She won't mind.'

'She mightn't, but I would. I'm looking forward to it — she's such good company.' She shrugged immediately she realised she'd implied he wasn't.

'If you're so determined,' he said, sounding rather petulant before he hung up with an exaggerated sigh, saying he'd call tomorrow.

Liz replaced the handset. 'I feel a bit mean. He sounded so disappointed.'

'Tough. Hayden does take you for granted, Liz. You've got a lot to learn about men, even after surviving the Moody mayhem. It's not a bad idea to let them know they don't always have to be around for us to have a good time.'

She'd declined to accommodate Hayden's wishes. Had the inheritance given her confidence a boost, or had the high she'd been on all day ambushed her thinking processes? Hayden Grant was a man of substance, a man she cared about. Dismissing her uncertainty, she went to her wardrobe and chose her classiest dress.

An hour later and Liz tapped impatient fingers on the dressing table. 'Angie, how much longer before you're ready? You look lovely, really you do, that rich burgundy silk does something for your skin and dark eyes.'

'You never know, tonight might be the night I meet Mr Right. It's worth a few extra minutes isn't it?'

Liz smiled. 'I thought we were having a girls' night out?'

'Sure, but I've always worked on the 'Be Prepared' principle.'

As Angie took a lingering look in the dressing table mirror, the doorbell rang. 'I'll get it. It could be Hayden, but he's wasting his time, if he thinks I'm going to change my mind,' Liz said with her new found confidence.

Swinging the door open, the placating words she'd say to Hayden on her lips, Liz was startled to find a stranger standing there — a casually dressed stranger. He wore a dark T-shirt, denims and trainers, had bronzed arms, was tall with sun-tipped hair.

'Can I help you?' She tried to keep her voice even.

He stepped forward. 'Elizabeth Shepherd?' he asked smiling widely. He'd

17

caught her totally by surprise in asking for her, yet she noted his A-list smile, the tonal quality of his voice, and her heart did an uncomfortable little jig.

'What do you want?'

The navy blue eyes pinned her down. 'Am I speaking to Elizabeth Shepherd?' he repeated.

She was now irritated, felt uneasy as she faced him. She'd heard about people pestering winners of lotteries. Surely the news of her inheritance hadn't started to circulate already. 'Excuse me? I don't think that's any of your business. If you're here to sell something . . .'

'I'm not a salesman, but your defensiveness tells me you are Ms Shepherd.'

'Who is it?' Angie called from inside.

Ignoring Angie, Liz said firmly, 'Nonsense, I'm not being defensive. I want to know who wants to see Ms Shepherd and why, and if you're not prepared to answer, then good evening.'

Angie arrived to stand by her side,

took one look at the hunk and nudged Liz enthusiastically.

'I'm a reporter from the local newspaper. All I'd like to do is come in and ask you a few questions.'

Angie intervened, obviously afraid Liz planned to discourage their good-looking visitor. 'We'll be happy to answer any of your questions. Fire away,' she said.

'So I was wrong. You're Liz Shepherd?' the reporter asked, giving her his fantastic A-listed smile.

Angie nodded as she attempted a return smile in duplicate. 'How can I help you?'

As Liz turned to glare at her friend, she received a quiet wink, and went along with the joke. Angie couldn't help herself sometimes. She wasn't about to let a man as good-looking as this one get away without checking him out.

'Perhaps I could come in? It's not the kind of thing we should be discussing on your doorstep.'

Liz frowned in Angie's direction, but

she was already saying, 'We're about to go out for dinner. I'd ask you along, but you're not dressed for the Hyatt.'

'My bad luck, eh? You really do look stunning, Ms Shepherd.' He paused, his gaze slipped across to Liz, and hesitating long enough for her to regard it as a courtesy, not a compliment, he added, 'both of you, of course.' He shifted from one foot to the other in an impatient gesture before going on, 'but I know you'll spare me a few minutes before you leave.'

Pulling a compact notebook from the side pocket of his jeans, he added, 'You're obviously celebrating something pretty special. It wouldn't by any chance be your inheritance?'

2

Liz gasped. 'How do you know about that?' she demanded. With a satisfied glance the reporter turned to Angie.

'Your friend's body language is most revealing. Congratulations on your good fortune.'

Liz felt hot, her stomach churned. How could she have been so undisciplined after she'd promised Mr Bowlen she'd respect old Tom's wishes not to make his legacy public yet? But before she could express her dismay, Angie jumped in, and jutting her chin, said, 'I'd like to say thanks, but I can't, because, alas, I haven't inherited anything, so if that's why you're here, it's sorry I have nothing to say.'

'Come on, Ms Shepherd, give me a break? You seem like a woman who'd enjoy the publicity. Old recluse leaves his millions to beautiful but penniless young woman? It'll make a great rags-to-riches story, and when readers see what a fabulous looker you are, they'll be fascinated.' He went to move off. 'Let me get my camera, it's in the car.'

Liz laughed cynically. 'Hold it right there. I don't like what you're suggesting. So, you'd be well advised to leave now.'

He swept a glance in her direction, his deep blue eyes glinting with impatience. 'That's very big of you, particularly as I wasn't addressing you. I was speaking to Elizabeth.'

'Look,' Angie burst out, 'You've got this all wrong. I'm . . . '

Liz stepped on her foot, and thankfully Angie got the message not to tell him he had them mixed up.

Angie took a breath and kept the pretence on the boil. 'Angie and I are in complete accord here. I've told you I haven't inherited anything. Please,' she waved one arm, 'interview over. Take your notebook and leave. Good evening, Mr . . . er . . . I don't believe you even bothered to mention your name.'

'It's Steve,' he said as he dived into his pocket and produced a business card. 'I don't understand why you're afraid of a bit of publicity. If I'd had the good fortune to inherit a few million out of the blue, I know I'd be shouting it from the roof tops.'

He raised his shoulders, tilted his head, as if he didn't care anyway. 'Should you change your mind, I'd appreciate a call. Human interest stories always go down well with the readers.'

'Sorry we can't help on this occasion, but we'll keep you in mind if we hear of a dog biting a man . . . er, Steve.' Angie sounded impressively patronising, not sorry.

As he turned towards the stairs, he muttered in a tone that could clearly be heard, 'What a couple of go-getting women. About what I expected.'

Liz and Angie stood in silence until

he was out of hearing. And only then did they dare to look at one another and burst into floods of laughter.

'We're not very nice, are we? He'll be furious when he finds out,' Liz said as they dropped into chairs inside, kicked off their shoes and put up their feet.

'He won't find out. It's so unlike you, Liz. What made you decide to have a bit of fun with him?' Angie asked.

Liz shrugged, uncertain why she'd made the hasty decision. 'Impulse really, and maybe we shouldn't have done it, but I thought the longer we put him off, the longer I'll have to find out how he knew about Tom's generosity. He'll probably be back if he thinks it's such a good story. Tomorrow I'm going to call his editor. Publicity is the last thing I want, as it would let the old man down. Angie, would you mind being me if he or any more newshounds come knocking on our door? I get annoyed and you're so good at one-liners.'

'Mind,' Angie said, grinning, 'it's the nearest I'll ever get to being an heiress.

Besides, if it means being in touch with that Steve again, count me in. Did you hear him say I look stunning?'

Liz smiled. 'Stop pretending you're fooled by his obvious attempts to win you over. Fact is, you do look stunning, and he was right when he called you smart, but you can stop with the nonsense that you think he's OK. You know he's up to something.'

Angie grinned. 'And we sent him off with a thistle in his ear, didn't we? Are we still going out for a night on the tiles?'

'I think it's a flea.'

Angie punched Liz lightly on the arm. 'Being an heiress doesn't give you the right to be such a 'know-it-all'. Flea or thistle, they'd both drive you mental.'

Smiling, she said, 'By the way, I really cringe when you call me an heiress — it sounds so glossy magazine, celebrity stuff — and I'm not an heiress. I'll settle for lucky.'

'OK, how does Lucky Liz sound?'

Liz smiled. 'It's an improvement. But to be honest, I'm worried. How did that reporter guy hear about old Tom?'

'Maybe someone from the legal firm blabbed, but your best friend is here to deal with him.' Angie's dark eyes shone with amusement. 'I hope he shows up again so I can have fun playing him along for a while before I burst his big ego.'

'Don't forget he's a reporter, he could get back at us,' Liz warned, but she was thinking it wouldn't do any harm to go along with the charade until she found out more about him. He'd mentioned he was from the local paper and it was known to beat up stories, sometimes unnecessarily, with emotive language.

Some years ago she'd found old cuttings from the daily papers with headlines that labelled her father, *Failed entrepreneur with grand visions*. She'd come across them when, months after her parents died in a motoring accident, she'd finally forced herself to sort through their things. Those head-lines had to be a beat up, for her father was a struggling mechanic dogged by bouts of depression and heavy drinking. In disgust, without reading them, she'd torn them up and flung them in the bin.

Angie interrupted her thoughts. 'Yes, or no, are we tripping the light fantastic, or has Steve's little visit upset our plans?'

'He's not going to put a damper on our plans, no way.'

Putting their shoes back on, taking a quick glance in the mirror to check themselves out, they left the apartment in party mood, but in the taxi Liz started to question if her good fortune was indeed lucky. The arrival of the reporter and any subsequent publicity he generated could turn out to be a major hassle.

As the cabbie drove into the pull-off outside the hotel, Angie poked her in the ribs. 'We're here, so clear old Stevie boy from your head and forget Hayden for a while. We're here to party.'

It brought Liz back to the present with a thud. As they alighted from the taxi she touched her friend on the arm and said happily, 'With you for company, why wouldn't I enjoy myself? Bye bye Hayden, bye bye Mr Reporter, at least for tonight.'

They laughed as they entered the restaurant and wine bar, but they hadn't booked a table and the restaurant was full. To their wails of disappointment, the young waiter suggested an upmarket place within walking distance.

As they strolled into the romantically-lit dining area, Angie whispered, 'It looks pretty posh.'

'For once we can forget about the money. Remember, I'm Lucky Liz,' she responded light-heartedly, as they were shown to a table overlooking the City Gardens draped in fairy lights. But her buoyant mood soon dissipated when she heard someone call her name. Angie leaned across and lowering her voice said, 'Don't look now, but I think that's Hayden I can hear. Have we seen him, or do we make a quick getaway to the ladies?'

Only now did Liz realise how much she'd been looking forward to a relaxed night out with Angie, but even if she were tempted by her friend's suggestion, she simply couldn't do it to Hayden. Whipping up a smile, she hissed, 'We'll make the best of it for now, but I'll insist we're having a girls' night out.' As an afterthought, she managed to fit in, 'Smile, and remember, don't mention the legacy,' before Hayden was by their side. His lips were warm on her cheek, a whiff of alcohol teased her nostrils.

'Well ladies, this is indeed a pleasure. I thought I'd be eating alone.'

You will be, Liz told herself, quite determined. 'I thought you said you were going to *Forbidden Fruit*.'

'No, I said we were going, Elizabeth. I'd planned a special evening for just the two of us.' He gave Angie a glance of dismissal. 'I'd even booked a table. I was so disappointed when . . . '

Did Liz detect a slight slur in his voice?

A hovering waiter stepped forward. 'Would you like another chair at the table, Sir?'

'Thank you,' Hayden said. 'You don't mind sharing her with me tonight do you, Angie?'

'Of course not,' her loyal friend said, making light of an awkward situation. 'Any friend of Liz's is a friend of mine.'

He smirked at Angie. 'The same goes for me,' he said, obviously trying very hard to be pleasant, as he took the chair now placed between the two women.

A Hayden smirk wasn't something Liz saw too often. And though it confirmed her belief that he'd had too much to drink, it surprised her. He liked to be in control, and the thought that he'd been drinking alone affected her.

'Drinks?' he asked in a jovial voice.

'Yes, please, a white wine for me.'

Angie's dark eyes gleamed, telling Liz she intended to enjoy herself, Hayden or no Hayden.

To Liz the thought of a drink sounded just the ticket to ease her sense that the night was about to get tricky, but she needed to keep her wits about her. 'I'm not in any hurry, are you, Ang?' she asked, unwilling to risk kicking Angie under the table to warn her to agree. 'Hayden, have you been here long?'

'A while. I called in for a quick drink on my way home.'

'A quick drink or three, I'd say,' Angie chipped in with a laugh. 'Drowning your sorrows because Liz let you down tonight, eh?'

Liz glared at her. Hayden muttered something inaudible, and typical Angie, having said too much, sought to clear the air. 'Actually I'm starving. Why don't we order first?'

'Good idea.' Hayden snapped his finger and thumb in the direction of a waiter, who hurried across with the menus and handed them around. They ordered and Hayden suggested, 'While we're waiting we'll have champagne — your best.'

'I'll ask the drinks waiter to bring it across, Sir.'

Shortly after the champagne arrived in an ice bucket, the waiter opened it and poured Hayden's flute for tasting. He approved with a nod of his head and soon Liz's and Angie's flutes were filled, and Liz's best intentions had vaporised.

When the waiter departed, she said with a frown, 'Why champagne, Hayden? Are we celebrating something?'

'Of course we're celebrating.'

Angie straightened in her chair. 'How on earth did you find out about the legacy?'

Liz held her breath. Even the subdued lighting couldn't hide Angie's face that now glowed with the guilty colour of crimson.

'Sorry, I've put my foot in it again,' she said, dropping her head to pretend a renewed interest in the menu, leaving Liz and Hayden facing one another.

He raised his eyebrows. 'What legacy?'

Liz sighed, her hands felt sweaty, as she tried to toss off the news with a casual response. 'I was going to tell you tomorrow, but you may as well know now. Today I learned I've inherited a house and . . . '

Hayden made some perfunctory remarks, lines of amusement forming around his hazel eyes. 'How nice, Elizabeth. An old aunt's little place in the country?'

His patronising tone really annoyed her. 'As a matter of fact it's a mansion called *Wellington Grange* not far from our apartment. You may even know of it.'

Her attention wrested from the menu, Angie looked up and her face beaming, added in an excited voice, 'And it's gotta be worth at least five million. From now on, I'm calling her Lucky Liz.'

Hayden moved to the edge of his seat, Liz could hardly fail to see the hurt in his eyes. 'I don't appreciate you making fun of me.'

She felt cold. 'It's true, Hayden. I wouldn't make fun of you, you know that.'

'But you're quite happy to let me find out by accident. It says a lot about our relationship, doesn't it?'

Privately, Liz agreed, but now wasn't the time to deal with it. 'I'm sorry. My feet have hardly touched the ground since I heard about it. I did think about ringing you, but you've told me so many times you hate being interrupted at work.'

'And when I asked you out to dinner, you didn't bother to mention it then?'

'I wanted to tell you in person. The law firm asked me not to talk about it. Hey, you're making me feel as if I'm being questioned in the witness box,' she said, attempting a smile while reminding him his attitude didn't impress her.

His tone softened. 'Sorry. It's a habit. Did you mention the firm who's handling the will?'

'Bowlen & Bowlen.'

He nodded. 'Reliable. I don't recall you ever speaking of a wealthy aunt or uncle.'

'No, my benefactor is a friend. I've referred to him a few times. Tom Lawson was such a sweet old guy.'

'Who apparently has no family. You certainly know the right friends to have.'

Again, he tested her patience. 'You're my friend. Does that include you?' she snapped.

Angie cut in, 'Liz was very good to him, Hayden. Probably kinder and more thoughtful than any son or daughter he may have had. That's why he left her his property.'

'You're right to point that out, Angela. I'm sure Elizabeth was. It's just that from my experience in practising law, when it comes down to it, blood is thicker than water. The relatives nearly always inherit. But this is good news, so let us drink to it.' And raising his glass he said, 'To Elizabeth who is not only beautiful, but has a generous heart.'

'To Lucky Liz,' Angie added as they clinked their flutes together.

Wracked by a storm of unsettling thoughts, all Liz wanted to do was slug it out with Hayden and get it over. But this wasn't the time or place to deal with something as major as their relationship, so forcing a smile, she drank her champagne and forked through her meal. Her appetite had forsaken her.

They made uneasy conversation over the main meal, with Angie throwing in the occasional humorous remark, and to Liz's surprise and relief, Hayden excused himself before dessert. 'You're not driving?' she asked.

'No. I'll get a taxi. I'll call you, Elizabeth.'

Anxious to spend time alone with him to sort out their obvious differences, she suggested, 'Let me cook dinner for you tomorrow night and we can talk.'

'I'll go out and leave you guys the place to yourselves,' Angie said.

He tilted his head. 'Good evening and thank you ladies for your company.'

They watched him, tall, straight and respectable, as he strolled to the door, Angie drawn to comment, 'What a splendid exit for someone a bit under the weather. Did his body language say goodbye or what?'

'He's a proud man and I've upset him. I should have told him about the legacy instead of offering excuses. We are supposed to be a couple.' She sighed. 'I don't know why I didn't.'

'Don't you?' Angie said quietly.

'Not really. He's very good to me. Now all the gloss has gone off this morning's good luck.'

'I'm going to spoil the party a bit more. Liz, deep down you have to examine the real reason you didn't tell him. Hayden is too full of himself, he's got too much confidence, too much presence. I understand why you go out with him — given half a chance I would too — but bottom line, he's a control freak, and you tend to let it wash over you. You have to face it. If he's not in charge, he's not interested. Can you cope with that?'

Liz gave a weary smile. 'Oh, come on, he's not that bad. He's a lawyer, an advocate. It's in his nature to manage things. I'd far rather have a man of mental strength than one who doesn't know what he wants and can be manipulated.'

Angie tilted her head. 'OK, but he's not your manager. And I hate to point it out, but did you notice how he lightened up when you told him the inheritance was substantial?'

'You told him that, not me, my foot-in-mouth friend, and yes, I noticed. But, so did you when we were told.'

Angie placed her hand on Liz's arm. 'Excuses, excuses. All I'm saying is, you're about to become wealthy, and wealthy women are vulnerable to men who have a fondness for money.'

Liz sighed. 'I know you mean well, but Hayden is more interested in success than money, and I've had one bad experience with a man, so stop worrying. I'm not likely to make the same mistake again.'

Angie, as always, eased the serious tenor of the conversation. 'Auntie Angie wasn't around to wise you up when Mark Moody was on the scene. Otherwise, I'd have picked that phoney a mile off.'

Liz forced a smile. 'I think Hayden was genuinely hurt that I didn't share my news with him straight away.'

Angie hit her head with her hand. 'And I didn't help, blundering in and telling him about the legacy. I'm a disaster in high heels.'

'Forget it. We all made mistakes tonight. Oh well,' Liz sighed, 'I guess things will work themselves out. They usually do.'

Angie raised her shoulders in a

gesture of uncertainty, 'Are you going to ask his advice about *Wellington Grange?*'

'If he offers. I know you're ambivalent about him, but I trust him. He'd never try to cheat me out of anything.'

Angie tilted her head. 'I happen to agree with you about that, but there's one more thing I'd like to add to the mix before we finish this conversation. Prepare yourself for an offer of marriage soon.'

A knot developed in Liz's already unsettled stomach. Marrying Hayden had suddenly become a subject she preferred not to think about.

'Where did that come from?' she asked.

'The house. I can see him living it up in that house, you giving dinner parties for his friends and legal contacts. It's a temptation he won't be able to resist. He'll get you and . . . '

'Enough!' Liz held up her hand. 'I don't want to hear the rest. Can we go home?'

In the taxi home they commiserated about the celebration which had turned into a let-down, but decided on another girls' night out soon. And by the time they reached their flat, they were chatting and joking as if the night had been a success.

Liz yawned as she pushed open the door. A note had been tucked under it, and reaching down to retrieve it, she sensed it wasn't going to be good news.

'What does it say?' Angie urged, leaning over her shoulder.

Unfolding it, she read aloud. '*Dear Ms Shepherd, Sorry if I was rude to you earlier tonight. I'll contact you tomorrow to arrange a meeting. — Steve Lewis.*'

Waving the paper, Liz raged, 'Can you believe the nerve of this guy? He still thinks I'm going to talk to him.'

Angie raised her brows. 'That's me he's addressing, and I might just say yes to the handsome hunk,' she said, grinning.

'I'll admit he's good-looking, but so

are cuddly koalas and when angry we know how dangerous their claws can be. If he has the gall to phone, I intend to give him a piece of my mind. But he probably won't because first thing tomorrow morning, I'm contacting his editor to complain about his intrusive behaviour.'

★　★　★

During a break in activities at *Fantastic Flowers* next morning, Liz hurried to the hospital coffee shop, ordered a drink and in a quiet corner, tapped out the number of the local newspaper Steve Lewis worked for. It took some doing to actually get the editor to talk to her, but eventually a gruff voice boomed down the line, 'Yes, what is it?'

His manner made her stiffen her back.

'Sir, I had a visit last evening from one of your reporters. I didn't appreciate him calling without phoning first, nor did I . . . '

'Nonsense, woman, my reporters don't work evenings, except by appointment.'

'I assure you Steve Lewis came to my place looking for a story after six o'clock.'

'Madam, what kinda story?' he barked.

'That's not important. I'm complaining about Mr Lewis' rude manner.'

'You're mistaken, madam. I don't have a Lewis on my staff,' he thundered into the phone and hung up.

Liz stared at her phone, frustration surging through her. Appalled as she was by the fact that the editor's manners were even worse than Mr Lewis', it was what he said that really stung her. Lewis didn't work for the paper. And she couldn't dismiss his visit as a practical joke, for he knew both her name and that she'd inherited something.

Who was he and what was he up to?

3

Liz thought of Hayden. Maybe he'd have some ideas. She dialled his phone and, as usual was frustrated by being asked to leave a message. She tried to muster up an assertive voice and said, 'Hayden, it's Liz. I expect you for dinner tonight. We have to talk. Call me if you can't make it, otherwise I'll expect you at seven. Bye.'

On her way back to *Fantastic Flowers*, Steve Lewis was very much on her mind. As she walked through the main entrance, in the distance, a man standing at the hospital reception desk arrested her attention.

She frowned. She'd seen him before at the hospital, and somewhere else. She shook her head. It couldn't be him. This man was wearing expensive business clothes.

Not completely convinced, she decided

to risk it and try for a closer look. How, without being seen when she had to pass by the desk to return to the shop? As she neared him he appeared to be in earnest conversation with the clerk. Drawing in a long breath, she held her hand to the side of her head and hurried by. And just as she thought she'd made it and expired a long sigh of relief, his voice halted her.

'Hello there. It's Angie, isn't it? I was hoping I'd bump into you. You got my note?'

She turned automatically, though the wiser thing would have been to keep walking. Her heart pulse lost its rhythm. What the devil was Steve Lewis doing here? Coincidence, or was he following her? Trapped into responding, she glared at him as he strolled in her direction. In business clothes, she conceded, the man looked very presentable, but it only increased her animosity.

'Yes, I found your note, but I'm not even going to pretend I understand why you think I'd want to meet you again.'

He smiled, his unusually dark blue eyes teased. 'Don't pretend people haven't told you you're very attractive. Why wouldn't I want to meet you again?'

Her face flared. 'I'm not stupid. I don't believe for a second that's your reason for asking me to meet you.'

Again, he caught her by surprise. 'You're Liz Shepherd, aren't you? Don't bother to deny it. Why did you try to pass yourself off as your friend?'

He's guessing, she thought, though the embarrassment of yesterday's hoax accentuated the heat glowing in her face. 'What makes you think that?'

'Maybe because I can imagine an old gentleman, any old gentleman, being, shall we say, captivated by you.' His appreciative glance travelled over her. She felt desperately in need of a put-down response to win back some of the high ground.

'Frankly Mr Lewis, your imagination is running wild. Yesterday you were

Steve Lewis, reporter, but today . . . '
she braved a sweeping glance over him,
adopted a sarcastic tone, ' . . . you're
Steve Lewis something else by the look
of your clothes. So who are you really?
The editor of the local paper certainly
hasn't heard of you.'

'That's his loss,' he said with a
confident tilt of his head. 'He doesn't
know what a good story he's missing.'

'Tell me what the story is,' she
challenged. It made no sense to a girl
who normally disliked males who
thought their good looks and confident
smiles gave them permission to be
pushy.

'I'm happy to, but the middle of a
busy hospital corridor is hardly the
place for a serious conversation. If you
have time for a coffee, I'd be happy to
explain.'

'I've just had a drink, and you know
what? Suddenly I'm not interested in
any explanation you might give. I'm
due back at the shop,' she snapped,
though beneath her irritation lurked

47

curiosity — a desire to hear that explanation.

'You own the flower shop?'

'Excuse me? You know where I work?'

'I saw you coming out of *Fantastic Flowers* a while back. Fantastic name.'

Fantastic smile, she thought, begrudgingly.

'Let me compliment you, you have a very nice little business.'

'Mr Lewis, I think you're on a fishing expedition to find out if I own it or not.'

'Ms Shepherd, you overestimate your importance. Why would I be interested in what you own or even where you work?' he said smoothly. 'I just happened to glimpse you leaving the florist shop earlier.'

Liz felt vaguely disappointed, shrugged. 'Yet you seem very interested to find out more about why I inherited *Wellington Grange.*'

Oh, blast, she thought, he had her so confused, so anxious to hold her own in the conversation, that she'd told him

48

exactly what he wanted to know.

'Congratulations. It's a charming old house and the money will be handy. You must be excited by your good fortune.'

'You know about the money, too?'

As he nodded his honey-coloured hair danced across his forehead. 'Yep. What good's a lovely old house with no money to repair it? A family member left it to you?'

'No,' she said sharply, 'and your earlier reference to old men tells me you know that.'

A voice called across to him from the reception desk, 'Mr Lewis, we have that information for you.'

'Thank you,' he replied before turning back to her. 'If you can't make it for coffee, dinner tonight, Liz?'

Don't encourage him, she told herself. Walk away now and he'll get the message, yet she lingered. 'Why? So you can ply me with questions about the legacy?'

'You don't like me very much do

you? If you have dinner with me, perhaps you'll discover I'm not a bad bloke after all.'

Yes, his invitation tempted her, but she managed to summon the strength to say, 'Sorry, I already have a date.'

'Another night, then? There are a few issues to clear up between us, such as my knowing about your good luck, and you and your friend trying to put one over on me. Let's not wait too long before we talk.'

Drawing in a sharp breath, she tried a careless tilt of her head to dispel any impression that he made her uncomfortable. 'Call me, I'm in the phone book. I think we could have a very interesting conversation.'

Grateful that she no longer faced him, she ran a finger over her flushed cheeks. What was Steve Lewis' interest in her and the legacy? An unwelcome idea came to mind. Suppose he was a developer interested in buying the property to turn it into apartments, or, heaven forbid, to pull it down to build fashionable, yuppie townhouses?

But her exchange with him disturbed her on another level. She'd read in his navy blue eyes as they glanced over her, appreciation, guarded appreciation. How did she feel about that? Her heartbeat told her she didn't mind at all, but she couldn't allow her heart to control her actions.

She knew nothing about Steve Lewis and she'd already been burned by Mark Moody when she'd given in to her heart. Steve was clearly up to something and if it meant going out to dinner with him to find out what, she'd do it.

Inside the shop, she flicked strands of hair from her sweaty forehead and took another long breath. Flowers, floral arrangements and fussy customers were not uppermost in her mind as she worked, trying to put Lewis out of her thoughts and analyse her feelings for Hayden. If, as Angie suggested, he might ask her to marry him, she wasn't ready.

And while her thoughts kept boomeranging back to Steve Lewis, she had no hope of deciding anything about her future. The man intrigued her. Today she'd even found him vaguely charming. His early brashness as a reporter was obviously an act, and the dinner invitation and promise to explain things had a sincere ring to it. Actually, she conceded he no longer came across as someone with a smart mouth.

Somehow she managed to get through the day without making any serious mistakes or any serious decisions. When it came to closing the shop, she still hadn't heard from Hayden. She'd really upset him and should call him again to apologise, but stretching, she quickly succumbed to the idea of a quiet night at home.

But before going home, she phoned the Bowlen legal firm and mentioned Steve Lewis' activities. 'Do you know why this man should be interested in my good luck?' she asked.

'The name Steve Lewis doesn't ring

any bells. I'll look into it and get back to you, but meantime you'd be advised to give him a wide berth,' Bowlen Junior said. 'These things shouldn't happen, but sometimes minor staff members talk to their friends about their work. That's maybe how your Mr Lewis heard about your inheritance. It's unlikely, but you have to consider he could be a con man who plans to talk himself into a share of the property.'

Liz laughed. 'If that's what he has in mind, he's going a very funny way about it, posing as a loud-mouthed newspaper reporter. The only thing he's talked himself into is my bad books.'

'Keep it that way. You'd be wise to get advice from someone you trust, just in case. You mentioned Hayden Grant as the person who'll handle your legal work in the handover to the estate?'

Liz had quite forgotten. 'Yes, but I haven't spoken to him yet.'

'Do it straight away, and inform him about this Lewis chappie. If necessary he can take some legal action to sort the fellow out. By the way, I was about to contact you. We've taken control of all the old man's papers, but someone has to visit the house and sort through his personal effects — clothing, household goods, etc. For a small fee we can arrange to have that done if you wish.'

Liz had a vision of someone totally detached from old Tom, throwing everything into a pile and dumping it at the tip.

'No. I'd prefer to do it myself, with your agreement of course. I'll visit at the weekend. Is the power still connected to the house?'

'You can pick up a set of keys any time and I'll have the electricity switched back on for the weekend,' Michael Bowlen said in what sounded like a relieved tone.

Arriving home, weary, Liz stumbled up the stairs and inside, put on the kettle, made a cup of peppermint tea and placed a frozen dinner in the microwave.

While eating, she propped up a

photograph of *Wellington Grange* and smiled. Was the beautiful old home really hers? Might she live in it? Might Angie move in with her? Might Hayden ask her to marry him? Don't think about that — concentrate on the other things — she told herself.

After clearing away the debris of her meal, she flopped into a comfortable chair with her picture and drifted off to sleep.

Angie's call, 'Liz, is it safe to come in?' woke her.

Her friend looked around the room. 'Hayden didn't show?' she asked.

Liz shook her head. 'Didn't even phone. He must be seriously upset. Cup of tea?'

'Good idea. Stay there, I'll put on the kettle. It looks as if you've really done it with poor old Hayden for the time being. But I wouldn't lose any sleep. He'll be back. It won't only be your personal charm and five star looks that lure him back. It'll be that bank balance you're about to accumulate.'

Liz tilted her head. 'Angie, there might not be a bank balance. I could decide to spend it on doing up *The Grange*. Besides, Hayden isn't like that.'

'Your Mr Grant likes to impress. He enjoys a quality lifestyle. It all costs money.'

Declining to acknowledge Angie's word, she changed the subject. 'Guess who I bumped into this morning? Steve Lewis.'

'Wow. No kidding. Where?'

'At the hospital. I don't know what to make of that man. He was wearing business clothes, actually looked managing director material, and sounded reasonable. The startling thing is he wasn't fooled by us yesterday. According to him he knew I was Liz Shepherd from the start. In retrospect, switching our identities was a stupid idea anyway. I wish we hadn't done it. Now he probably thinks I'm flighty, capricious.'

Angie shrugged. 'And I was thinking of giving up my day job so I could play you. Anyway, do you care?'

Liz tilted her head. 'He didn't actually say it, but he makes me feel uneasy about inheriting the house. Don't ask me why, but he does. He promised to explain his odd behaviour if I had dinner with him.'

Angie gestured with her hands. 'Well, there you are. What better excuse than that for going out with him?'

Liz shrugged. 'I'd really like to hear his excuses, but I'm a bit ambivalent.'

Angie raised her brows. 'Oh come on, Liz, you're dying to have dinner with him.'

'The lawyer said to avoid him, even suggested he could be a con man.'

'Oh spare me, con men have shifty eyes and smooth tongues. Steven's dark blue eyes are fabulous and he has a fondness for tossing insults around. If he were setting out to con you, he's using a very odd technique.'

'That's what I thought. I've been wondering if he's a property developer who wants to get hold of the house so he can turn it into apartments. What do you think?'

Angie stifled a yawn. 'Maybe.'

'Am I keeping you up?' Liz asked.

'Can we discuss this tomorrow, Liz?'

She smiled. 'Yes. Unfortunately, the problem will still be here.'

★   ★   ★

It was late next afternoon when Liz, the keys to *Wellington Grange* in her hand, strolled up the overgrown gravel path to the tessellated tiled verandah, her heart pulsing with anticipation. She still hadn't heard from Hayden, but again she'd put off contacting him, for the pull of the old house was stronger than any guilt she felt. Angie had offered to come with her, but somehow in deference to Tom she decided to make this first visit alone.

Gently, she eased open the heavy stained oak door with its brass knocker, and hesitantly stepped into the long hallway. Though it had the musty smell of abandonment, the gracious old home filled her with poignant reminders of a lonely old man. And as she moved from room to room, the eerie silence, the chill and gloomy shadows of its emptiness, its closed drapes and blinds shutting out the world, emphasised the isolation in which Tom had lived his final years.

There were no photographs, no signs of any presence, not even that this was once a vibrant, bustling home, filled with people and music.

Unnerved, she forced herself towards the heavy wardrobe in the main bedroom, dreading the moment when she opened it, for she would come face to face with a powerful expression of Tom's friendless existence. No-one had bothered with him. Would anyone want the clothes of an old man?

As she reached into the wardrobe, she hesitated. Was that a sound she heard at the front door? She persuaded herself it was the autumn breeze playing with a loose roof tile. But suddenly a sense of foreboding enveloped her and closing the closet, she decided she wasn't yet up to going through Tom's possessions.

The next time she came she'd throw open the curtains and invite the sun into the house first. She'd ask Hayden to accompany her. It had been a mistake to come alone, she was hearing things, imagining things. She paused, stood very still. There it was again, this time the sound of a door shutting. Her feet felt frozen to the spot.

When a voice called, 'Hello, where are you?' startled, she turned quickly, almost falling over her own feet, but before she could answer the owner of the voice stood at the door of the bedroom.

Astonished and furious, she lashed out, 'Mr Lewis, what are you doing creeping around this house? You have no right to be here. If you followed me . . . ' Seizing her mobile from her pocket she went on, 'I'm reporting you to the police for harassing me.'

Lewis came forward, smiling, though his voice sounded concerned rather than relaxed. 'No need to do that. I didn't mean to frighten you. Look, I'm real, I'm not a ghost.'

'I didn't suppose you were, but I do think you frightened me on purpose, and you're trespassing. I'm putting an end to this one way or another.' Finger poised over the phone pad, she shrilled, 'Do I ring the police, or do you tell me why you're so interested in my movements?'

How she managed to sound forceful when she felt so confused and uncertain, she had no idea, but impressed with her performance, she planted her feet firmly on to the once gleaming floorboards and waited for his response.

'I promised you an explanation the other day, but you refused my invitation.'

'I had to get back to my job.' Her forcefulness had lost some of its passion.

Steve Lewis felt as if he were treading

hot coals. He knew he'd find her here. In fact he'd followed her, as she suspected, but fool that he was, he'd failed to arm himself with a reason that she'd accept once he made his presence known. He'd blundered in unprepared and really put her offside. How ham-fisted could you get?

'Do you have time now, or are you too busy sorting through your newly-acquired possessions?' Blast, he hadn't meant to sound so cynical.

'This isn't the first time you've hinted I'm a gold-digger and I don't take kindly to it, you obnoxious man,' she said angrily.

Her defensive and quick response really surprised him. Of course he wanted to know if Liz Shepherd had used her feminine wiles to persuade the old man to leave her his estate. But on first and second meetings she'd seemed incapable of such a materialistic act. Now, he wasn't sure. Women who beguiled old men out of their money had to be coldly calculating.

Was Liz Shepherd shrewd as well as beautiful? There's no urgency, wills take time to be processed and you've made a bad start. Whatever you do, keep her onside, try to get under her guard. It's the only way you'll ever find out the truth.

By the way apology, he said, 'Sorry, if that's the impression I gave.'

'You make a habit of it, and to quote old Queen Victoria, I am not amused,' she said in a calmer tone as she sat on the edge of the bed.

Taking advantage of her quieter mood, he followed quickly with, 'So do you have time to talk?'

'I'll make time,' she said tilting her determined chin. 'But I warn you, your story will have to be good.'

Steve believed her. Her green eyes gleamed with spirit when she challenged him. The fairly temperate person he'd first met was today really fired up. He'd have to remember not to give away his own feelings.

'There's a conservatory at the back of

the building, I believe. We could talk there,' he suggested, his thoughts jostling for a credible story to give her — it had to be acceptable, believable.

She moved towards the door with an elegance he'd noted before. She wasn't tall, but her trim figure gave the impression of height and grace, and he guessed she frequented a gym.

Reaching the door, she swung back to him with a smile laced with contempt. 'How do you know there's a conservatory at the back?'

He'd made another elementary slip. He had to get himself together and stop thinking of Liz Shepherd as a woman.

'Don't all places like this have a conservatory?'

She shrugged, stood aside for him. 'Lead the way, then.'

They entered the conservatory with its half-circle of windows looking out upon what had once been a formal garden, but in the ascending gloom looked sadly weary and overgrown.

'It's quite dark in here. Would you

mind turning on the light?' Liz asked.

Steve obliged and triggered the switch that illuminated the area with several ceiling lights.

She strolled across to the windows, turned and stood by one of the cane chairs, setting one of her legs forward of the other.

'You've been in this house before, haven't you, Mr Lewis?' she demanded.

He ran his hand through his hair. 'Excuse me? That's an odd thing to say.'

'Is it really? So how do you explain that you knew about the conservatory?'

'I've already told you.'

'Not to my satisfaction, and if it's the way you're hoping to explain away the fact that you knew exactly where the light switch was in here, don't waste your breath. You can't brush off my question with a nothing reply. As the soon-to-be owner, I insist on knowing when you were last in *Wellington Grange*, and what your connection with it is, Mr Lewis?'

Steve's gut knotted, he tugged at the

neck of his T-shirt, the muscles in his face felt like straining elastic. He wasn't used to playing a part. Where to from here?

'Perhaps you'd better sit down,' he said quietly.

She spelt out her reply. 'I do not want to sit down. I'll stand, thank you very much.' And with frightening authority, she added, 'This time make your answer credible.'

'I'll sit myself, if you don't mind,' Steve said, feeling as if a rug had been pulled from beneath him.

'Sit all you like, Mr Lewis, but start talking, and make it the truth. I've listened to your lies long enough. I'm usually a together person, but believe me if I get really worked up I can be quite daunting. When were you last in this house and why?'

Steve Lewis eased into a chair, shook his head, flourished his hands in a gesture of frustration. 'I'm afraid it's rather boring.'

'Boring I can take. Lies, I can't.'

He shrugged. 'I should have realised you'd guess. It's true. I've been in the house before. Once I knew it very well — I lived here as a boy. That's what brought me back to this area.'

4

Liz felt breathless. Her glance swept over him, seeking any body language, anything that would tell her he was making this up. She read only sincerity in his deep blue eyes. Nevertheless, he'd lied to her before, and even if he had once lived here it didn't answer all her questions.

'Your family owned *Wellington Grange*? When? What?'

Waiting for his answers, she felt a little unsteady and decided sitting down was sensible, and dropped into the dusty old cane chair opposite him.

'My mother owned it. My father gave it to her as a present before he walked out on us. I would have been about eight or nine. As I said, it's not a very interesting story, kids miss out on having a father all the time. But for me it's a sad story.'

If the manner in which he lowered his eyes wasn't enough to tell Liz he still hurt over the loss of his father, the sober intonation in his voice did.

'I'm sorry,' she said. 'Having a father around is something I enjoyed as a child, though my dad wasn't the life of the Shepherd family. He was often depressed and drank too much.' She halted, offered an apologetic smile. 'Sorry, this conversation isn't about me. You said you lived here for a while. Why did you move on?'

'My mother couldn't afford the upkeep or to employ any help. It was far too big for her to care for on her own and we didn't need all the rooms. Mum used to tell us it was built in the early nineteen hundreds by Sir Adrian Bartels who had a cricket team of children and a football team of servants.'

For the first time he smiled. The memory had obviously prompted a moment of pleasure. Liz was seeing a side to Steve she hadn't experienced before, and within the composed and self-assured exterior, she decided lurked warmth, and even a softness she could admire.

She folded her hands in her lap, engaged in his story. 'And your mother, where is she now, and any siblings? A sister or brother?' she asked.

'A younger sister. We went to live in England and later Melanie found herself an older, wealthy Californian, ten gallon hat, spurs and all that, and settled down with him. Mum, who had struggled all her life, joined them in California. I visit as often as I can. Crikey,' he said dashing back his hair, 'It's my turn to apologise. I haven't talked so much about the family in years.'

'Thank you for telling me. You studied in England?'

He nodded. 'Yes and got on with my career,' he said simply. And crossing to a large potted plant, he fingered its dusty, once shiny leaves. 'These plants could do with a drink. Perhaps we could water them now?'

It was a nice thought, but her trust not completely restored she wondered if it was a diversionary tactic? He hadn't told her what his career was, where he lived, or how he knew about the inheritance.

'It's a good idea, but first, indulge me once more. How did you find out I was about to inherit the house? It's been puzzling me ever since your quite convincing imitation of a rude journalist.'

He smiled, waved his hand as if brushing off a trifle. 'It wasn't hard. I called at the local property agent to enquire about *The Grange*. It's a property agents business to know all the significant homes in the area. The woman told me the owner had died recently and she'd heard on the grapevine he'd left it to a young woman who had befriended him. I should warn you, you're on her list.' He tilted his head, his confidence restored, 'She's planning to call on you as soon as the will's processed to see if you want to sell.'

Liz frowned. 'But she doesn't know I've inherited it, so how did you? You're not trying to avoid answering me, are you?'

'No pretty lady, I happened to be in the vicinity of the house when you wandered by.'

'Oh come on.'

'I was sitting in my car surveying the old place, reflecting an old times, when a very attractive young woman happened by. You looked a little uncertain as you opened the gate. It was almost as if you felt you were trespassing, but you went in and wandered around the garden and I just knew. I could tell by the smile on your face, the glow in your green eyes, you'd just inherited the house and you loved the garden.'

She laughed gently, allowing herself to enjoy what was clearly a compliment. 'If you saw all that, I'm surprised you didn't mention what I was wearing.'

He smiled appreciatively and with his

reply kept the game alive. 'I could tell you what you were wearing, but why ruin my romantic first picture of you with such mundane things as clothes?'

A feeling of pleasure swept over her, his captivating manner had started to divert her away from the subject. They weren't supposed to be talking about her. Quickly she said, in a quiet tone, 'I understand now how you knew from the start Angie and I were misleading you about our identities. Afterwards you followed me to our apartment and pitched me that line about being a journalist. You already knew I was the beneficiary?'

Displaying one hand, he said, with a trace of embarrassment, 'Guilty. Yes, I followed you home. Later I decided to call at your house to make certain who you were.'

'Are you a journalist in real life?'

He laughed. 'Was my performance that good?'

'Absolutely convincing.'

'If I've answered your questions to

73

your satisfaction, shall we water the plants? I think we can find a watering can or a dipper around here somewhere.'

Though still unsure how she felt about him, she decided to go along with his idea. Later he might tell her more. 'Yes. Let's get into it.'

Perhaps for half-an-hour they ferried water in two pails from an outside tap to the indoor plants in companionable silence before he took her bucket from her and set it down. His warm hand touched hers. Her heart missed a beat.

'That's enough for you for one day,' he smiled down at her. 'It's heavy work. Let me finish it off.'

'No, no,' she insisted, trying to ignore his dark glance gliding over her. 'There are only a couple more.'

He shrugged. She tried to ignore the broadness of his shoulders, the strong arms. 'You're the boss,' he said.

'Ha.' She reclaimed her empty bucket and marched back to the tap.

He laughed, did another trip with a

full bucket before standing aside and watching her struggle part way back with hers, before relieving her of it. She brushed hair back from her hot cheek and submitted to his superior strength.

'All done,' he announced, giving the last hanging basket a drink, and turning to face her. 'But they're going to need more than this light drink. If you agree, I can call and check the garden's watering system to see how well it operates tomorrow. The whole garden looks in need of some TLC.'

The idea appealed. That was the problem. She'd started to notice Steve as a man, to see him as more than attractive, to feel uncomfortable when he came close to her. And she had far too many loose ends in her life to start falling apart because a man she hardly knew looked good and had a smile to die for.

'That's thoughtful of you, but I have to decline.' She wove an acceptable excuse through the minefield of her emotions. 'Officially the property doesn't belong to me until the legals are finalised.'

'You should hurry things along,' he urged, closing the outside door. 'The place is going downhill fast.'

It reminded her that she hadn't yet asked Hayden to act for her. 'You're right. I've been so preoccupied with my good luck, I've neglected the necessaries.' Judging it prudent to let him know she had a boyfriend, she added, 'The man I'm going out with is a lawyer.'

'Get him on to it. It shouldn't take long.'

She smiled. 'I will. And now I must be off.' As they walked towards the front door, she made conversation to ease her discomfort. 'Did you enjoy living here?'

He paused. His dark eyes surveyed her. 'They were the happiest days of my life. After Mum and Natalie moved to the USA I missed them and started thinking of those days.' He shrugged. 'That's what made me develop a yen to come home and have a look at the old place.'

'So do you plan to settle in the area? Have you found a house?' she continued as they reached the front door.

He tilted his head. 'I think you know the answer to that.'

Oh dear, she thought, I wish I hadn't asked that question. He sounds really serious about buying *Wellington Grange* and I don't think I want to sell.

But she was immediately distracted when, about to place the key in the door, behind her the front gate squeaked and scrunched open. Turning quickly, to her consternation, she saw Hayden striding self-importantly down the path.

Unedited, her words came out, 'Hayden, why didn't you call me yesterday? What happened?'

He ignored her question as he drew up to them. 'Angie said I'd find you here.' And turning to Steve, he said in his best lawyer's voice, 'And you are?'

Steve proffered his hand, 'Steve

Lewis, and you?'

The handshake lasted only the time it took for Liz to turn her attention from Steve to Hayden.

'Elizabeth's legal representative. I hope you're not here looking over the place, my friend. It's not for sale, is it, Elizabeth?'

Liz stared at Hayden, but when Steve replied quickly she held back her critical response.

'That's a matter for the owner and me. I'll call you again, Liz, if I may?'

She nodded. 'Thank you for your assistance today, and your explanation.'

'My pleasure. And I meant it about the watering system.'

He acknowledged Hayden with an angled head and ambled off to the gate.

Taking a long breath to gain her composure, she kept the door ajar. 'I haven't made up my mind about selling. You obviously have, Hayden. Normally a man with your training would want to see the house before making up his mind.'

He smiled. 'Wise counsel. Perhaps I can go through it now? By the way, it's good to see you,' he said, his warm lips brushing across her cheek. 'I'm sorry if I sounded overbearing, but that guy wouldn't have the money to buy this place anyway. And you are going to ask me to represent you, I hope?'

She pushed the door back open. 'Yes. I planned to ask you last night, but when you didn't bother to ring,' she protested, stomping down the passage to let him know she wasn't impressed, 'I thought you weren't interested.'

'I had an horrendous day. But I called in to your apartment as soon as I could.' He caught up with her, spread his hands. 'I say, you're very fortunate. This has been an elegant old home in its day.'

As they visited room by room, Hayden inspected the condition of the walls and ceilings, the light fittings, and furnishings with interest.

'You're impressed?' Liz asked, weary, but determined not to hurry him. She did, after all, want his advice.

'Very,' he said, 'with some refurbishments, it could be returned to its original grandeur and be one of the most significant homes in the area.'

She shook her head. 'It sounds wonderful, but I don't know that it's wise to spend the money on those kinds of alterations. It would really cost. I'm not sure how to proceed.'

He placed his arm around her waist. 'If I sell my place, that will give us the finance to do it.'

Liz stopped short. 'Excuse me? Aren't you getting little ahead of yourself? I'm asking for your advice, not your money.'

Hayden moved closer to her. She felt uneasy, breathless. 'I'm not offering you my money. I'm suggesting we get married.' And tilting her chin with his finger so that their eyes met, he added. 'Now that you've got this beautiful home, there's no reason for us to delay marrying any longer.'

Forced to look into Hayden's eyes,

Liz saw how green they glistened. And as his lips found hers, she asked herself if she'd seen in his eyes love for her or enthusiasm for what she would bring to the marriage.

Her stomach churned. Angie's prediction that Hayden would ask her to marry him echoed in her mind.

She slipped Hayden's finger from her chin, avoided his eyes, but folded her hand into his, anxious not to disconnect with him. As Angie said, he liked to control things and he had a streak of snobbishness, but he'd always treated her as a lady, been attentive and appreciative of her.

She was not from the high society set in which he moved, she had no eminent connections or university degrees, yet he didn't knowingly patronise or make her feel inadequate or small.

Hayden probably loved her, so why wouldn't her unexpected legacy prompt an earlier proposal than he'd planned? She couldn't explain it, even to herself, but in her heart she knew she didn't love him in the way she had imagined true love would impact upon her.

'Hayden,' she said quietly, releasing her hand. 'This is rather sudden. I need time to think about it. Is that all right?'

He looked crestfallen. 'I thought you knew I loved you. But take all the time you want.' He paused there, smiled. 'I mean by that, a day or two. The sooner we get started on the renovations . . .'

It was typical of Hayden. 'So the renovations are more important than my feelings,' she said using an amused tone.

He turned to her, waved his arm around, as if prosecuting a case. 'You see what this house has done to me? I'm mad about it.'

She continued to tease him. 'I hope you're as mad about me?'

He picked her up and swung her around with boyish enthusiasm. 'Much more. You're beautiful, practical, considerate. I know I'm not one to show my feelings on the outside, but I love you. When do I tell the partners at the practice that we're getting married?'

She laughed, hardly able to believe his display of emotion. If she wasn't very careful, she might find herself saying yes. She called up the strength to reply, 'As my representative, can you make contact with Michael Bowlen and find out what has to be done to finalise the handover of the property? Once that's settled we can start discussing our future.'

His hazel eyes gleamed. 'But we are engaged?'

She pointed to her ring finger, anxious not to be corralled into a corner from which there was no escape. 'I don't notice a diamond.'

'That's easily fixed. We'll go shopping tomorrow. I'm glad you prefer dia-monds. That would be my choice.'

Uncomfortable and definitely not prepared to commit to marriage, she also felt guilty that by postponing her decision, she may be leading him on. She shook her head. 'Really, I was joking. So much is happening right now, I don't think I can cope with a marriage proposal or an engagement. If I learned one thing from my mother, it was that life-long commitments should never be rushed.'

And turning on her heels, she strolled back to the front door to avoid more questions. 'If you've seen enough, we should lock up and go.'

He caught her up. 'I should warn you I don't give up easily.'

That's part of the problem, she thought, continuing her way to the door. As a lawyer, persuasion was part of his stock in trade.

As she locked up, he said, 'You didn't say who that fellow was with you earlier? I hope he wasn't making a nuisance of himself?'

'He used to live here. He was interested in looking through the place for old times' sake.'

'I don't like the sound of that. A complete stranger and you let him into the house?'

'Not really. He came inside. I didn't

invite him,' she said.

'Are you sure he hasn't got a secret agenda?'

'Such as?'

'Elizabeth, you've just inherited this beautiful property. Surely it's occurred to you he could be up to no good?'

She laughed. 'You lawyers, you're such a suspicious lot. Michael Bowlen suggested something similar.'

'It was good advice. We're only looking out for you. How did this fellow find you, anyway?'

She sighed. 'It's a long story, but I'm satisfied with his explanation.' Why was she defending Steve Lewis, she wondered.

'That's fine, I'll make the time to listen. I'd like to hear this long story,' he said.

She forced a smile. 'You're making me feel as if I'm in the witness box again.'

More of Angie's words came back to trouble her. While Hayden's penchant for controlling things often amused her now, if she were to marry him, living together, she felt sure would soon start to irritate.

'You said his name was Lewis. What does he do?'

She shrugged. 'I don't really know. I didn't ask.'

'For someone you don't really know, just now you seemed rather friendly.'

'You're not feeling a little jealous are you?' She attempted a change in emphasis. 'I've never known you to be jealous.'

'And I'm not now, but I did resent the way he looked at you.'

His suggestion upset her heart rhythm, but she refused to let it influence her. 'Hayden, you're imagining it. He's almost a stranger.'

'Men know about these things. He's mentally noted you down as attractive, perhaps even desirable. Not that I can blame him. You're beautiful and you have a lot of class.'

Liz couldn't believe Hayden's unrestrained mood, how endearing she found it. 'Thank you,' she said, resisting an urge to curtsey.

'My pleasure.' He glanced at his watch. 'Can we continue our discussion this evening? I have a client to see now. I'll drop you off at your place.'

'Thanks, but I'll enjoy the walk,' she said. 'Will you come for dinner tonight?'

'Yes. We need to make plans.'

'Hayden,' she reminded him, firmly. 'I haven't agreed to marry you. I'll expect you at 7.30 tonight.'

'Did you give me the name of that big guy?'

'Yes. Why?'

He shrugged. 'I'm interested.'

'I introduced you. He's Steve Lewis, but I don't understand your interest.'

'I'm looking after your interests. I'm not altogether satisfied with his explanation that he once lived at *Wellington Grange*. It's too much of a coincidence that at exactly the same time as you've inherited the house he shows up.'

She smiled. As usual, Hayden was turning an ordinary event into a prospective legal challenge. She could see nothing sinister in the timing of Steve Lewis' arrival.

'Coincidences probably don't happen in court cases, but in real life they do, Hayden.'

He seemed unaffected by her casual attitude. 'See you at 7.30 tonight.' His brief kiss was neither passionate nor possessive. Angie would have called it a 'husband-type kiss.' Alarmed at the idea, she hurried off before his car left the kerbside.

He'd planted so many conflicting thoughts in her head and she was determined not to spoil her inheritance by questioning everything. She needed Angie's take on today's events.

★ ★ ★

'Hayden asked you to marry him? Didn't I tell you he would?' Angie said in an excited voice as she and Liz sat down for a chat over a cup of tea.

Liz smiled as she curled into an easy chair, drained by her lively afternoon. 'I hope you're not going to claim to be psychic?'

'You don't have to be psychic to reckon that guy knows his onions. If you say yes, he gets a smashing looking woman and a beautiful old house and bags of money. Imagine him playing lord of the manor? He was never going to turn his back on that opportunity. Did you give him an answer?'

Liz tried not to let the enormity of her decision bog down her thoughts, and responded light-heartedly, 'No. I wanted to talk it over with the oracle first. What's your honest opinion?'

'I'm glad you haven't said yes. You're only twenty-four. You're unsure about this marriage — that's obvious — so why rush into it. The only thing that's changed is the legacy.'

'My mother, if she were alive, would remind me Hayden has all the qualities a good husband needs, and if I let him go, I might never find another man like him.'

Angie leaned forward in her chair. 'My guess is, in your heart you don't really want a man like him, do you? And the house introduces a new factor into the equation. You have your own security now. It opens up an endless number of options for you — travel, a florist shop of your own, a once-in-a-lifetime holiday are just a few. Hayden's got a lot going for him, but first I'd do a bit of living. Liz, if the man really loves you, he'll hang around.'

'I doubt it. He's already talking about refurbishing the house. He's even suggested selling his own apartment and paying for the renovations.'

Angie sighed loudly. 'For goodness sake, be firm. Don't let him take over your life. Tell him you're not ready.'

On edge, Liz eased herself forward in her chair. 'The fact is the legacy has complicated my life. It was a fabulous gesture from old Tom, and I don't want to sound ungrateful, but until it happened my life was going along very nicely.'

'Oh come on, Lucky Liz. You don't mean that.'

She threw up her hands. 'I'm suspicious of Hayden's motives and Steve Lewis' attention, and it didn't help when he turned up at the house this afternoon.'

'The dishy Mr Lewis showed up? That guy's either crazy about you, or just crazy. What excuse did he give for arriving unannounced this time? It'll have to be good for me to believe it.'

Now, unsure what to think, Liz admitted, 'It is an unusual story. He once lived at *Wellington Grange* as a child.'

'Oh, spare me the details. He sure knows how to spin a great yarn.'

'It was obvious the house was familiar to him. He knew where all the rooms were. He led me straight to the conservatory.

'His father deserted the family and went overseas, before leaving *The*

Grange to his wife.'

Angie tilted her head. 'As delicately as I can put it, I think he's pitching you a sob story. Where would he get the money to buy a property like that for a start?'

'He didn't actually make an offer, but I had the feeling that's what he was thinking.'

'Before you get involved with Mr Lewis, find out more about him, what he does, where he lives, what his financial situation is, and why he's following you around.'

Liz raised her voice. 'Angie, I am not getting involved with him. I wish you wouldn't keep suggesting I'm falling for the man.'

'You could have fooled me. If I were you, I wouldn't be worried about Hayden. He's easy to read. You know what you're getting there. It's Steve Lewis who's hijacked your attention and that, I'd be very concerned about.' Angie turned towards the bedroom, leaving Liz standing with her mouth open. Could Angie be right?

5

Hayden arrived on time, carrying a bunch of exquisite yellow rosebuds and a bottle of fine white wine. Liz graciously accepted them and his brief kiss, thinking, not for the first time, that he was a man who knew how to please a lady. He had so much going for him so why didn't her heart beat just a little faster.

Over the meal, they skirted the subject most on their minds by talking generalities — he about his office comings and goings and she of work at the florist shop. He enquired about Angie and surprised Liz by saying, 'She's such good company one tends to overlook her physical appearance — I couldn't help noticing the other night how brilliant her dark European eyes are, yet she seems unaware of it.'

'She's very attractive, but then I'm a

woman, so my opinion probably doesn't count. But what I like about her most is her ability to be a loyal, entertaining friend. She's great fun to be with, but she's also very observant and can be serious. As a matter of fact . . . '

She was about to say it was Angie who predicted his proposal to her, but she thought better of it. 'As a matter of fact, I'd love to find a man worthy of her.'

'Perhaps she's looking for a hot-blooded Italian,' he said with a touch of amusement.

'She'd take a hot-blooded man of any extraction, so long as he's genuine and loving.'

As she poured the coffee, she suggested, 'Let's drink it in the lounge. We might as well be comfortable while we talk.' The knot in her stomach told her these uneasy delaying tactics were getting them nowhere, and as Hayden hadn't raised the subject of his proposal she would have to do it.

Settled in a chair opposite him, she

took a long breath and began, 'Hayden . . . ' at exactly the same moment as he said, 'Elizabeth . . . '

They laughed uncomfortably. 'You first,' he said.

She began hesitantly. 'Thank you for asking me to marry you. I'm flattered, very flattered, but it's come as rather a surprise, at a time when I need space for other things.'

'We've been going out for six months, surely it wasn't that much of a surprise.'

'But you'd never even hinted at marriage. Your proposal caught me quite unprepared. I've given it a lot of thought since you asked and I find I'm not ready for marriage.'

He held the tiny coffee cup in his hand, making him appear larger, even more confident than normal. She felt a bit shaky, wondering exactly what he was thinking.

'Now let's examine this with clear heads.'

Her nervousness got the better of

her. 'I don't want to examine it. My head is quite clear, Hayden. Do you always have to sound as if you're in court?'

He looked positively crestfallen by her outburst. 'Elizabeth, I'm trying to help you. I understand you're nervous because this is probably the biggest commitment you'll ever make. I'm sure most women go through it after they've been proposed to. It's a big decision, but in a day or two you'll get used to the idea. I love you, Elizabeth, I always have, and I want you for my wife.'

She sighed as she sank back into her chair. How much easier it would be to buckle under his persistence and give in. Her heart raced as Angie's voice echoed in her head, 'Be firm. If you're not ready, tell him and make sure he understands all you're asking for is time.'

She found herself saying, 'I'm touched by your love, and your proposal, but the truth is, it wouldn't be fair to either of us if I accepted right now. I have so much on my mind with *Wellington Grange*. Let me get my head around that first.'

He drained the coffee cup, said evenly, 'Naturally I'm disappointed, but I'm prepared to wait until we decide what to do about the house. I can make it a priority.'

You're not listening, she wanted to shout, *I* will decide about the house, but he continued to speak. 'By the way, I've made a few discreet enquiries about that Lewis fellow who was at the house today. You did realise he was inspecting it, I hope? He's an architect, operates overseas, but planning to open a branch of his business here in Melbourne.'

Liz gasped. 'You found all that out in a few hours. How?'

'It doesn't matter how. The fact is you must be wary of him. He's hoping to get the property by deception.'

It surprised her to learn Steve was an architect, and yes it surprised her that she felt a need to defend him when he'd never been open or forthcoming about his background. Every detail she knew about him she'd received only through questioning him. And yes, Angie thought he'd made up the story about living at the old home and reminded her to be cautious. But getting the property by deception? It sounded way too heavy.

'If he wants to buy the place, if he operates a business overseas, why wouldn't he make me an offer? Why would he resort to dishonesty? It doesn't make any sense. Not to me, anyway.'

'There are some business people who only know how to operate dishonestly. That's what keeps them competitive. You're naïve about people. That's why you need me around to protect you.'

Dear heaven, she thought, I can't stand the pressure he's putting on me, and I have an uneasy feeling it's going to be like this until I agree to marry him.

'Unlike you, I haven't had much

experience in life, Hayden, but that doesn't make me naïve or stupid. I've talked to the man on several occasions, and if he is up to something, please leave me to handle it. It's my problem.'

He stood up and came to her side where he squatted on the arm of her chair and took her hand. 'Your inexperience makes you vulnerable and I find it and your innocence endearing. I'd hate you to change. I want to take care of you, Elizabeth. Won't you let me?'

She snatched her hand away, knowing she had never been more vulnerable than she was at this very moment — vulnerable to his plea; at risk of giving into him because she didn't want to hurt him; because to say yes was the sensible thing to do. Setting back her shoulders, summoning all her inner strength, she said, 'I can't. I must do what I believe is the right thing for both of us.'

He stood, for the first time appearing uncertain, even a little pale. 'Is there someone else? Does that Lewis fellow have anything to do with your sudden rejection for me?' he asked sharply.

'How can you call it a sudden rejection when you only asked me to marry you this afternoon? As for Steve Lewis, why would you think he has anything to do with it?' she said, flinging herself from her chair, grabbing up the coffee cups and stomping off to the kitchen.

He followed her. 'Because I saw the way he looked at you. I've spent enough time in courtrooms to know how people think from their body language and the way they twist words.'

Angry now, she raised her voice. 'So, like Angie, you too can read minds. I'm surrounded by people who see into my future and think without their help, I'm on the path to ruining my life.'

'If that's how you see it, I'm sorry. But I assure you, I have no doubt about Lewis. He wants *The Grange* and he wants you,' Hayden said imperiously.

Liz felt a rush of heat into her cheeks.

'That's rich coming from you. Isn't that exactly what you want? You didn't ask me to marry you until I inherited the house, did you?'

His face muscles tightened; he turned on his heel and strode to the door. There he paused. 'When you've regained your composure and given things a lot more thought, you'll see there's a vast difference between Lewis and me. Call me when you're ready and I'll set in motion the transfer of the house to your name.'

'I want it done straight away,' she shouted to his stiff, angry back.

The door slammed closed as she returned to the lounge room where she flopped into a chair and gave way to tears of frustration and disappointment. Why had it gone so wrong? Hayden liked to control things and she'd been mildly amused by it, but tonight she'd seen how wearing, how debilitating its effect could be. It really got to her.

★ ★ ★

101

Liz was starting to wish she'd inherited a holiday home. She'd have taken off for it at the weekend and considered never coming back, but by early in the week her head started to clear and she accepted that running away from the problem wasn't a workable option.

As she bunched flowers to display in the window of the florist shop, it came to her that for the moment she needed do no more than get the house transferred into her name. After that, she could wander through it, enjoy the ownership, the feel of the old place, before making up her mind how much it meant to her. And only then could she decide on her future. But first, as Hayden hadn't come back to her about the legal transfer of the house, she felt compelled to contact him and check on his progress.

She was about to use her mobile when it rang. 'Liz?' the now familiar voice asked, making her uneasy because, blast it, she felt pleased.

'Steve? How are you?' she said

hoping she sounded calm.

'Have you thought any more about my offer to put in a watering system at *The Grange*? With this continued dry weather, you're going to have to do something.'

'I've had more important things on my mind. Sorry, I haven't given it a thought.'

'You sound stressed. Problems? With the house?' He seemed interested.

'Partly.'

'Let me know if I can help. Meantime, it's been very dry the last few days. I hope you don't mind? I took the liberty of going over there and measuring up for a system. It won't be expensive and will keep the garden alive while you decide what to do with the house.'

For goodness' sake, was she so helpless that every man and his dog seemed to think she needed their help?

'I've changed my mind,' she snapped. 'I can look after it myself. And by the way, you didn't bother to tell me you're an architect?'

'Er . . . yes, I am, but I don't see the relevancy,' he said uncertainly. 'Except, I suppose, it explains why I felt competent to organise your watering system. I've designed several for large properties.'

Angie's warning that she should be concerned about Steve flashed into her head. 'Hoping to buy them?' she demanded.

'Some.'

'Mr Lewis, is that why you're hanging around me? You hope to persuade, poor naïve little Liz Shepherd to sell out to you at a bargain price?'

'Liz, why would I think you're naïve? Quite the opposite in fact. A naïve woman would never . . . ' Steve broke off, hastily decided it wasn't a good idea to say that only smart women inherited lovely old homes from sick, lonely old men who were practically strangers.

'Would never what? Suspect a nice man like you of having ulterior motives for being friendly with me? Well, I've got news for you — I do — so stop ringing me and trying to be so nice. I haven't worked out why, but it's clear your interest in me has strings attached.'

Steve's mind worked overtime trying to understand her change of heart after they'd parted on a friendly basis a few days ago. It probably had something to do with the legal eagle boyfriend who'd shown up at the house.

Suppose he'd been delving into Steve's past, trying to find out who he was and why he was so interested in *The Grange*? He shrugged. Good luck to him — the man wasn't likely to get any joy there. He'd only just arrived back in the country.

He softened his voice, enquired with concern, 'Liz, you sound really upset. What's happened to make you so unhappy with life?'

A long sigh came down the line. 'Last night someone called me naïve, and then you come on the phone today and start trying to run my life, organising watering systems and the like for me. Frankly, I've had it with men who think I don't have the intelligence to manage my own affairs.'

The boyfriend, the handsome but stuffy Mr Grant, must be the culprit. It didn't surprise Steve. The guy had a know-it-all style, an arrogant swagger.

'Liz, you need some fresh air. Could you get away for a while? Let me bring sandwiches over to the house in say, half-an-hour. We could stroll through it, get the feel of it. I could point out its architecturally significant characteristics. It might help you decide what you want to do with it.'

'It might,' she said uncertainly.

Could he persuade her? 'We could also use the time to discuss the watering system. That's really something that needs urgent attention if the garden is to survive. I'm not trying to run your life, Liz, I'm trying to be practical. And . . . ' he paused briefly, ' . . . I'd like to see you again.'

He could hear her breathing, almost hear her mind ticking over as he waited for her reaction. He desperately wanted to get to know her better, to tap into and understand what made her tick. But the difficulty was, that in the process, he was falling for her and that could spell danger if she turned out to be a woman without a conscience, an opportunist.

'Well,' she began hesitantly, 'I admit I want to go back to the house, and I could do with some company, not to mention some fresh air. OK, yes, I'll meet you there in an hour.'

'I'll bring lunch,' he said, pleased but unsure what had brought about the change in her mood. 'See you at *The Grange*.'

Liz's heart raced, she felt confused. Why did she allow him to talk her around so easily, she wondered, as she advised her boss she was going out to lunch? Melba didn't yet know of her good fortune — she'd delayed telling her until she decided how much the inheritance would affect her present situation.

★   ★   ★

Steve was sitting on the verandah step, waiting for her at *The Grange*, a large paper bag containing sandwiches and coffee by his side. He smiled as she strolled along the pathway. Again she thought what a fabulous smile he had.

Though Tom Lawson's solicitors, Hayden and even Angie had warned her to be wary of him, it was so easy to allow her heart to persuade her he didn't have a hidden agenda. He seemed genuinely attracted to her. She unlocked the door and as they passed inside, he propped it open with a handy coat rack. 'The house needs some air, too,' he suggested, 'it's been locked up for far too long.'

'You're right. A magnificent old place like this deserves better. I really must decide what to do with it. Shall we eat in the back garden? We can talk there,' she said, already feeling happier than she had since her spat with Hayden.

As they dusted off the old bench seat and occasional table and began eating the sandwiches, she asked, 'Would you mind answering a question that's been puzzling me?'

He laughed. 'Can I ask one in return?'

'You can ask,' she said flippantly before going on, 'Why did you go through that charade to meet the new owner of *The Grange*? Why didn't you come to me and ask if you could go through the old house you once lived in?'

He shrugged, bit into a sandwich. 'I was only guessing you were the new owner. I wanted to confirm that and see what sort of woman you were. If I'd known what an attractive and approachable young person you were, I wouldn't have hesitated to ask, but acting as a journalist seemed like a good idea at the time.' He grinned. 'Did I overdo it?'

'You were very convincing — a real turn-off,' she said with a curve of her lips. 'Now your turn.'

'Have you thought much about your plans for *The Grange?*'

'Why are you so interested?' she asked.

He raised his brows. 'Lately, I've been reliving the happy times I had here, and I'm tired of travelling the world, seeking contracts. I'd like to settle down. I could be interested in buying it if the price is right.'

Though his answer sounded reasonable, it didn't quite satisfy her. 'I suspected you might want to buy,' she replied, taking a drink from her coffee, 'and split it up into apartments?'

He glanced quickly at her. 'What makes you think that?'

'You're an architect. That's what today's architects do, isn't it?'

He smiled, swept his hand across the back of the house. 'They also restore old beauties like this one back to their former glory. If you decide to sell, I hope you'll advise me before you put it on the market. I've become very attached to it.'

'My dream would be to see it restored,' she said thoughtfully, 'if you could promise that, I may sell.'

'I'd love to restore it, but it's your house — it's up to you. Now, about the watering system, I've drawn up plans for your approval.'

As he reached into a pocket, removed a blueprint and unfolded it, it occurred to her that he had avoided answering her question. But her attention in a flash returned to the blueprint as he pointed out the features with long, lean fingers.

Her glance shifted to his face, the sun-tipped hair spilled across his forehead, his muscles eased and tensed as he spoke, detailing the diagram. When he suddenly turned his dark blue eyes upon her, he caught her intense gaze. She blushed.

'Shall we tour the garden while I explain what's going to happen and estimate the cost?' he suggested as if he hadn't noticed.

Embarrassed, she excused herself in rather a hurry. 'I must be getting back to work. I'm in my lunch hour. Steve I'd be happy for you to go ahead with the system.'

He laughed. 'You're in your lunch hour? What a remarkable woman you are. I bet you haven't even told your boss you're about to become a wealthy woman?'

Smiling ruefully, as they made their way towards the front door, she explained, 'I couldn't believe it was true in the beginning. I mean, I didn't know Tom owned the place, or had any money and now, well . . . I can't quite get around to giving up the shop. I love the work and the hospital location, but old Tom's generosity has made it necessary to rethink everything I've become accustomed to in my life. I hate to sound ungrateful, but in a way, Tom didn't do me a big favour.'

'Most women I know would quit

their jobs and be out there spending their inheritance like a shot. I take it old Tom was your benefactor?'

She nodded, grief tugged at her heart. 'Poor old darling. He was desperately lonely. He didn't appear to have any family or friends and lived a very frugal life.'

He leaned towards her. 'But he had you. That makes him a lucky guy.'

She tilted her head, a small smile touched her lips. 'You think so. I did what I could, especially after his first heart attack.'

'You knew he might die?' His question had an edge to it.

'I knew he was very ill, but as for dying? I didn't want to think about it.'

'And you had no idea he planned to leave you *The Grange*?'

She halted in the passage, frowned. 'As I just said, I didn't even know he owned it. Nobody around here did.'

'The real estate people did. I suppose you constantly ask yourself why an old man you hardly knew left you a fortune?'

'The solicitors said it was Tom's way of saying thanks for the small things I did for him.' She shrugged. 'It has an unreal ring to it, but what else could I do but accept it?'

They'd reached the front door. He touched her on the arm. 'Liz, he could have said his thanks by leaving you a few thousand dollars and you'd have been delighted, but this mansion, his bank balance? It's odd. And don't tell me you haven't thought about it. I sense you're not as comfortable about this as you pretend.'

She stopped, surprised by his insight. 'Of course I've asked why — it's like a haunting old tune — it keeps drifting through my head — but to be honest, something else about the inheritance disturbs me more. I'm uptight because I know people will think I deliberately set out to charm old Tom into leaving me his money. And,' she said heatedly, turning tear-filled eyes upon him, 'deep down it hurts. It isn't true, Steve.'

His resolve to stay unmoved wilted at the sight of her tears, and without thinking, he reached across, hugged her, fingered away a stray tear as it trickled down her cheek. 'Hush now, don't upset yourself.' His hand stroked her dark, glossy hair. He smelt the perfume of her, her body so warm and so close.

Stop, the warning bells in his head shrilled, this was not part of the plan.

He forced out the words to ease her pain. 'How could anyone think that of a lovely young woman like you?' But the knot in his gut twisted and his own pain shrilled out at him, you hypocrite.

Taking a long breath, he held her at arm's length. 'You're under pressure, uncertain what to do about the house and it's clouding your judgment, confusing you. Would you like to talk about it? Together we might be able to sort through the mire of ambiguities.'

Her eyes widened, she looked like a startled deer. 'You know that's exactly how I feel — under pressure, confused, uncertain. Even my closest friend, Angie, and Hayden, who's asked me to marry him, would scoff if I told them how insecure I feel about the legacy.'

'Liz,' he said, alarmed, 'surely you're not planning to marry a man who can't connect with your feelings?'

She sighed. 'Who knows what I'm planning. Certainly not me. I think I'll take you up on that offer to talk things through,' she whispered as she tucked herself back into the comfort of his arms. 'For the first time since I received the news, I feel hopeful I'll find a way through the multitude of doubts I have.'

'Let's have dinner tonight,' he suggested. 'You can talk all you like. To be honest, I'm looking forward to hearing more about your generous old benefactor.' Smiling, he released her. 'You'd better get back to work before *Fantastic Flowers* sends out a search party.'

Her lips curved gently. 'Alas, there are not enough people on staff to mount one.'

'About the watering system, I'll need access to the house to check out the plumbing and, if you agree, I'll arrange for a gardener to come in to cut the lawns and tidy up.'

'Let me know when you're going and I'll drop by with the key.' A suggestion of tears still glistened in her lovely green eyes.

'I don't want to put you to that trouble. I can call at the shop and get it from you.'

'Fine. Thank you, Steve Lewis. I never thought I'd say this, but I'm glad we met. You've been understanding and helpful.'

Steve gulped in air. She was so lovely, so absolutely adorable, and he'd fallen for her, totally. It wasn't how he'd planned it, but it served him right. He'd been too clever by half and now found himself locked into a situation from which he saw no escape. Unless he took her into his confidence, and to do that he'd have to tell her the very thing she dreaded most.

117

6

Liz's mobile rang as she arranged another sheaf of flowers for a hospital patient. Hayden said in his best legal voice, 'I have the transfer of ownership papers for you to sign.'

She decided not to get into a lengthy conversation with him. 'Thank you. I'll call into your office tomorrow.'

'I'd like to bring them around this evening if you'll be home. There's something I need to discuss with you,' he said, his voice softening.

As important as closing the legal arrangements on *The Grange* were, she didn't feel up to listening to Hayden press his case for marriage again. Going to dinner with Steve won hands down.

'I'm sorry I won't be home tonight. I'm happy to call into your office tomorrow if you name a time,' she said firmly, now following Angie's advice to be quite definite and not allow him to talk her around.

To her surprise he accepted what she said without question. 'If you insist. You're seeing that architect fellow tonight, I suppose?'

'As a matter of fact, I am. He's doing some work on *The Grange* for me.'

'Elizabeth, you do appreciate he's also doing some work on you? He's trying to ingratiate himself with you.'

On a long sigh, she snapped, 'Can we not go into that now, Hayden. Give me a time for tomorrow morning?'

If solicitors ever get petulant, that's how he sounded. 'Come before nine.'

★ ★ ★

Liz couldn't believe the excitement stirring within her as she made last-minute adjustments to her appearance. Dinner with Steve had somehow dominated her thoughts all afternoon.

The doorbell rang. 'I'll get it,' Angie called. Liz fiddled with one shoestring strap over her shoulder, waiting, almost breathless to hear his voice. But it was Hayden's legal tones that carried to her, and annoyed she stalked out, waylaying he and Angie in the hall.

'What are you doing here?' she demanded.

'I was in the area so I decided to call in, hoping to catch you to sign the papers. We don't want any more delays, do we?' Hayden's usual self-important manner had deserted him; his voice sounded almost apologetic.

A sense of remorse for her impatience swept over her. She should have felt flattered by his proposal, as she had as his partner during the months she'd gone out with him. Instead the inheritance had made her questioning, suspicious of his motives, suspicious of everyone.

'It was thoughtful of you,' she said.

Was that relief she saw in his eyes? 'Not at all.' He produced the papers, pulled out a chair for her at the table and handed her a pen. At her back, he indicated over her shoulder where her signature was required, explaining what it entailed and why. It took no more than five minutes for, when it came to legal affairs, she trusted him totally.

As he folded the documents into his briefcase, he said, 'I'd better be on my way. You look lovely, Elizabeth. Enjoy yourself.'

'She will,' Angie chipped in, saving her the necessity of replying. 'If you've got nothing better to do, why don't you stay on and have a drink, Hayden? I'm on my lonesome tonight.'

'Angie, I'm . . . ' he said as the doorbell sounded again.

Grateful that Angie had eased the uncomfortable atmosphere between them, Liz very definitely didn't want Hayden and Steve to meet. Grabbing her purse from the bedroom, she raced to the front door, calling, 'Thanks again, Hayden. We'll be in touch.'

She flicked back her hair as she opened the door. Steve smiled. 'Everything all right? Isn't that Hayden's car parked outside?'

She nodded, fingering her hot neck. 'Yes, he brought legal papers for me to sign regarding the title of *The Grange*.'

'Congratulations. It's one hurdle down. Now you can start thinking about what you want to do with the house.'

She shrugged. 'I'm not in any hurry. I want to get to know the house, wander through it, enjoy the sense of ownership for a while. Does that sound silly?'

'No wonder old Tom liked you. It sounds delightfully romantic.'

On the short trip to the Lygon Street restaurant, Liz tried not to compare Steve with Hayden. Steve's informality, his quiet air of assurance made her comfortable and relaxed whereas with Hayden she always felt on her toes, afraid she might do or say the wrong thing.

Seated in the restaurant, with drinks in hand, and their order taken, Steve asked, 'Do you feel like talking about old Tom?'

'Of course, but there's nothing really to tell. He was an old sweetie.' She laughed, 'Angie said he used to lay in wait for me to pass by the house after work, so he could buttonhole me for a chat. Maybe he did, but it was obvious he was terribly lonely.'

'You said old — as in sixty, seventy, ninety?'

'I've never really thought about his age. He looked old — as if he'd had a hard life — I guess he was about seventy-five.'

Steve cut into his steak. 'Did you ever meet any of his family? Family photographs — were there any on display in the house?'

'Yes, there was one of a family. I asked him about it and he told me it was his brother's family and they'd moved overseas. There really was nothing special about him, except he owned the big house, but I didn't know that at the time.' She teased, 'Are you sure you're not a reporter looking for a feature on the rich and lonely.'

He gestured with his hands. 'You could say I have the curiosity of a journalist. I'm trying to get a picture of a man who'd do something as generous as leave his entire fortune to, on your own admission, someone he hardly knew.'

Setting down her knife and fork, she looked hard at him. 'Every now and then I get the impression you don't believe my story. Why is that? No-one was more surprised than I was, I can tell you.'

'Maybe I'm pretending an interest as an excuse to have dinner with a beautiful young woman. Maybe I'm genuinely interested in a friendless old guy.' He laughed. 'To be honest, it doesn't make sense to me either. Did I tell you I've found suitable offices to set up a branch of my business in Melbourne?'

Liz's heart had begun to behave irrationally ever since Steve came on the scene. Now it did an excited little flip. 'That's great news. So you've decided to stay on out here?'

He smiled. 'That's the plan. I hope it means we can see more of one another.'

'I hope so, too,' she said quietly.

For the remainder of the evening they shared stories of their youthful successes and mistakes and laughed a lot. Liz couldn't remember ever enjoying an evening like this. On the way home she asked herself many time if he would kiss her when they said goodnight, and as they strolled to the door of her apartment she waited with breathless anticipation.

'Thank you, for a wonderful evening. Can we do it again soon?'

She smiled up at him. 'Yes, I'd like that.'

As he leaned towards her, her heart went on hold. But when his lips touched her briefly on her cheek, disappointment welled through her. 'It's been fun. Goodnight, Liz. I'll call you when I need access to the house.'

No kiss, no second date arranged. Liz couldn't believe how let down she felt, nor could she believe what she said next. 'I'm going to be at *The Grange* again tomorrow. If you care to call by around lunchtime, I'll bring the sandwiches and coffee.'

In the evening light he moved restlessly from one foot to the other. She felt hot with the thought that she'd embarrassed him. Red-faced, she turned to go in.

'See you at one o'clock tomorrow?' he said.

Inside, Angie, her dark eyes aglow with interest asked Liz, 'How did it go?'

'Wonderful.'

'Did he kiss you?'

Liz shook her head. 'A brief peck on the cheek.' She tried not to sound too let down.

'A Hayden-type kiss?'

'Exactly, Angie, a Hayden-type kiss.'

'Well, I'm pleased. You should get to know him better before you give him your heart.'

'Your good advice is getting rather boring. I'm not about to give my heart to anyone. How did your evening go?'

'Hayden and I had a ball. Can you believe it, he stayed on, and before we knew it, we were in the kitchen making pasta and salad and having fun at the same time. Did you know he's a good cook?'

Liz shook her head doubtfully. 'You had fun with Hayden? Angie, you're a genius. I had no idea he could cook, or have real fun.'

Angie laughed. 'He's so busy trying to impress people, he comes over as stiff and stuffy, but beneath it all I found a warm heart. Did you know he worked his way through law school? His parents couldn't afford the fees, so he found a job in a supermarket and worked his way up to senior stacking manager.'

Liz was preparing to go to her bedroom, but surprised, stopped and shook her head. 'Any time I asked about his parents he was non-committal. Perhaps he didn't want his background known to his colleagues.'

'Or to you? He's genuinely worried

about you, by the way, Liz.'

'Why?' she asked slightly irritated.

'He saw Steve going into the local government Planning Offices yesterday — and before you start accusing him of spying, they're in the building next to his.'

'And, later he just happened to pop in and using his legal hat, make a few discreet enquiries about Steve's business?' Liz scoffed. 'Is that how the story goes?'

Angie flopped into a chair. 'Gosh, Liz, you're being very defensive. Hayden is looking out for your interests. He is your legal advisor.'

'But he's not my keeper. Sorry, Angie, but the 'get Lewis' campaign you and Hayden are mounting is wearing rather thin, especially as it was you who suggested Hayden wanted to marry me because I'd inherited the property? Why is that suddenly OK?'

Angie's gaze pinned her down. 'Liz, I didn't say it was. The difference is Hayden loves you, he was always going to propose to you in time — inheriting the house simply changed the dynamics. Before we get too heated, why don't we make a cup of tea and have a chin-wag?'

Liz needed privacy to sort through her feelings. 'Not tonight, Ang, I'm tired and confused,' she said softly. 'Would you mind if we left it for now?'

'Whenever you're ready I'm here for you, you know that. When are you seeing Steve again?'

'We're having lunch tomorrow,' Liz said, and to stall more questions, she hurried off to her room.

Angie was right to advise her to get to know Steve better before she gave him her heart. Hadn't she learned anything from her ill-judged fling with Mark Moody? Since then she'd been wary of out-going, laid-back men. That's probably why she'd been drawn to Hayden with his conservative, old-fashioned values and manners.

That Steve Lewis. Why did he have to come along, filling her every thought with romantic ideas, making her heart pulse at the very sound of his voice, with anticipation every time the phone rang? She'd been so contented, so settled with Hayden.

Angie and Hayden seemed genuinely concerned about her and convinced Steve Lewis had a secret agenda. If she didn't at least give their concerns some thought she could lose their affection and their respect, and that mattered. She couldn't further the relationship with Steve, for which her heart yearned, until she knew everything there was to know about him.

Shaking off her shoes, she collapsed on to the bed, the way ahead as clear as a vivid summer sky. Tonight Steve had talked about his university days, building his business, the people he'd met along the way, but what did that really tell her about his family background?

Tomorrow she would leave her heart behind when she met him for lunch. She'd arrive absolutely fixed on finding out what made him tick, and why he'd turned up from nowhere immediately after she'd inherited the Lawson fortune. She'd insist on answers.

★ ★ ★

Steve Lewis couldn't sleep. He should never have imposed himself into Liz Shepherd's life. He'd done it with the best of intentions, in no doubt that the woman who'd been named in Tom's will was either an opportunist or an older busybody quietly hoping for a small legacy after his demise.

Those scenarios he'd have been able to handle, but when he discovered the recipient of the old boy's estate to be a generous-hearted, unsophisticated, lovely young woman, the idea that she'd duped Tom became tough to accept. He didn't want to believe it, yet how else could she have gained the house and money? Knowing what he knew about the old boy there was no way a man with his reputation would leave his money to her merely because she'd been kind to him.

The only credible explanations were, he'd had an affair with her, she'd taken advantage of an ailing and senile old guy and influenced him to make a new will, or she had something on him. And yet every fibre in his body told him Liz Shepherd was capable of none of these things.

If only he hadn't been drawn to her almost from the moment he met her. It had messed up his plans, presented him with a truck load of difficulties, and he'd handled things poorly, found himself in a very sticky situation, forced to tip-toe around the truth.

He got up, made himself coffee, went into the study and turned on the computer. If Liz hadn't worked her way into his heart, he could have challenged her assertion that she didn't know Tom was wealthy, demanded answers. Setting back his shoulders, he tapped in the search engine of the Web and waited. He'd have one more go at trying to understand Tom Lawson's motives.

★ ★ ★

At lunchtime next day, Liz made her way with determined strides back to *The Grange*. This was A-Day, the day she received straight answers. Steve waited at the gate, and held it open for her, but his usual smile was missing. He looked as uncomfortable as she felt. She hurried on to open up the house, uncertain.

'It's cool outside,' she said, trying to smile, wishing ironically that she felt cool inside. Instead her stomach felt like a boiling cauldron. This may be their last meeting. 'Perhaps we should eat in the conservatory,' she suggested.

He took the key from her, unlocked the door, stood aside, and gestured with his arm. 'For old time's sake?' It was the awkwardness with which he said it that confirmed to her that Steve, was uneasy.

As they settled into chairs and began lunch, Liz's heart pulsed so madly she blurted out, 'Steve, I . . . ' at the same time as he began, 'Liz, there's something I have . . . '

They laughed uncomfortably. 'Me first,' she insisted, afraid she might lose the impetus. 'Steve, I was about to say because I . . . ' her eyes lowered to the sandwich she held, her voice quivered, ' . . . because I like you, I've been prepared to accept most of what you've told me. I wanted to believe that you just happened to come along at the same time as I learned about *Wellington Grange*, but when I think about it, really think about it,' her confidence grew as the troubling questions she'd chosen to dismiss found voice, 'it's too great a coincidence to ignore.'

Was that concern that clouded his eyes? Was he about to deny her assertion? Her heart thumped, her face heated, but she pushed on, for to hesitate now might sap her resolve. 'I did a lot of thinking overnight, and I'm forced to the conclusion that your interest in this house goes beyond the fact that you once lived here. I won't be put off any longer, I have to know the truth.'

On the edge of his chair, he steepled his fingers against his chin in thought mode. 'Did you ever think I could be more interested in you than the house?' he asked. 'I can see the doubt in your eyes, but it's true. If you hadn't affected me so much, I'd have been able to satisfy myself within a day or two about your inheritance and have moved on or taken legal action. But . . . '

Liz stared at him. Ever since she'd known of the legacy, she'd been haunted by the thought that people would believe she had gained it by unscrupulous means. She'd even confided that to Steve, but now it seemed, that's what he felt, too. She cut in, her voice raised, 'Yesterday you were sympathetic, now you're taking legal action? Are you suggesting there's something illegal about old Tom's will?'

'Not about the will. I've no doubt that's lawful.'

Not a muscle moved on his face as he held her gaze. Her stomach knotted more tightly. 'If you think I cheated Tom, then I don't want to be here. I don't want to listen to your ugly accusations.'

She started to get up to leave, to get away from whatever it was he was about to say, but he reached forward and placed his hand on her arm. 'Stay, Liz, you will want to hear this. I'm sorry I didn't tell you earlier, but,' he shrugged, 'but I'm in love with you and under the circumstances . . . '

She remained on the edge of her chair, tossed her head. 'Say it. You think I duped Tom into leaving me the estate?'

He tilted his head. 'Tom Lawson was my father.'

Liz jerked up her head. 'Your father? I don't believe you. You've told so many lies about who you are and what you do, and I've been fool enough to believe them. But this time, you've gone way too far.'

Steve stood up, walked to the back of his chair. How she longed to beat her fists on his chest and demand he stopped lying to her, but she steadied herself, took a long breath and rising, walked towards the door with as much dignity as she could summon.

'Don't go, Liz. I understand why you doubt me. I haven't been as open with you as I would have liked, but I had my reasons, and now that you know who I am, you deserve to know why I've acted as I have,' Steve said quietly. 'After that, I won't bother you any more if that's what you want.'

She turned, glared at him, unable to come to terms with the disappointment, the forlorn recognition that again she'd been taken in by a man with a captivating manner, but no substance.

Unable to lie and tell him she couldn't care less what his reasons were, she faced him across the room. 'This had better be good. I don't know why I'm wasting my time.'

Returning to her chair, she was about to sit down when the full implications of his claim that he was Tom Lawson's son hit her as a savage blow from behind. If Steve Lewis was Tom's son, that made him the rightful heir to the Lawson estate. It was too much to contemplate right now.

'I've changed my mind,' she said in a hurry, 'I don't want to hear any more until I talk to Hayden.'

★ ★ ★

Before she entered Hayden's building, Liz took a quick look in her compact mirror and tried to repair the tell-tale signs of tears from her face. She could not allow her emotions to take control.

Hayden rose as she walked into his office. 'Liz, sit down,' he was sounding official, but not unkind. 'How can I help you? It sounded urgent.'

Tilting her chin with determination, she spoke the words she'd rehearsed on her way there. 'Steve Lewis is claiming to be Tom Lawson's son. If it can be proven, I wish to transfer my inheritance across to him. Will you handle it for me, please?'

Hayden leaned forward, resting his arms on his impressive desk, his brow puckered with concern. 'Did I hear you correctly? You surely can't mean you want to hand over the estate to Lewis?'

Of course he'd be aghast at any idea of signing away her inheritance. In her heart she knew that, but in her present mood she wanted it over, done, so she could walk away from Mr Lewis and the whole affair with a clear conscience. 'That's exactly what I want,' she snapped, 'and don't say I told you so. If it's any consolation to you I admit you were right. Mr Lewis had a hidden agenda.'

Hayden rose, came around to her side, where he propped on his desk. 'I wasn't going to remind you, Liz. I can see you're very emotional.'

'I'm not emotional,' she said through

misty eyes. 'I'm fed up. How soon can you validate his claim and get rid of the thing? I never sought or wanted the estate, it's brought nothing but guilt and unhappiness.'

'First we'll have to establish Lewis' identity and then . . . ' He gestured with his hands. 'Well, the fact is Tom Lawson left everything to you. You have to ask yourself why, if he had family.'

She gave a long sigh. 'Hayden, I've already asked that question a million times and I'm not satisfied with any of the answers I get. And you know what? I really don't care any more. Steve can have it all and the quicker the better so I can get back to being Liz Shepherd, florist.'

'Elizabeth, I understand your frustration, your disappointment, but have you thought about the man who so generously left you everything? If he'd wanted his son or any other family member to inherit that's how he'd have made out his will.' His hand covered hers. 'First allow me to confirm Lewis' claim of the relationship. Meanwhile, I want you to sit tight. If, indeed, they are father and son we can take it from there; consider making him challenge the will through the courts.

'Now,' his hand tightened around hers, 'I want you to go home and try to forget everything that's happened in the last week or two. Go back to the florist shop, have a night out with Angie and leave everything to me.'

His kindness brought a flood of tears. She sank back into the soft leather of the chair and let it happen. He handed her a handkerchief and returned to his desk.

'Thank you,' she managed to say as she dabbed at her ace, 'I must look a right sight.'

'You always looked good to me,' he said. 'No need to rush away. Take your time. I'll get on with this report.'

As she reached the office door, he called her name. She turned.

'I'll fix everything for you. I hope we're still good friends.'

She nodded, afraid to speak lest the tears at the back of her eyes spill over once more. He was such a nice person. Why couldn't she have fallen in love with him?

7

Liz spent Saturday at *The Grange*. When she handed it over to Steve, she was determined it would be as clean and as tidy as she could make it. During the day, in a drawer she found a bundle of yellowing newspaper clippings that looked destined for the garbage bin, but decided to go through them while she rested with a cup of tea.

Carrying it into the conservatory, she settled in a chair warmed by a patch of winter sun, and was about to reach for the clippings when she heard footsteps. Before she could do more than look up, Steve Lewis stood at the open door.

'You,' she gasped, almost upsetting the mug of tea as she jumped up. 'I thought you got the message last time that I didn't want to see you again.'

'There are too many things between us left unsaid, Liz. I couldn't let it go at that,' he said as her green eyes turned to ice. They spoke words such as liar, rotter, schemer, as they appraised him. Inside, the ache in his stomach felt like a volcano about to erupt.

How had he let the situation come to this? He should have trusted his instincts and walked away once he met Liz. Heaven knows he owed his father nothing, but refusing to question his motives, he'd continued to see her. Big mistake!

Did he really believe she was a young opportunist who had duped his old man into leaving her his fortune when the estate should rightfully be his mother's?

Single-handed she had raised Steve and his sister after their wealthy father abandoned them. Even *The Grange* he'd left them had been mortgaged. But he now believed Liz was exactly what his father had described her as — generous and thoughtful. And that she didn't know of old Tom's wealth until his death. He owed her the truth, down to the last detail.

He stood by the door, restless, uncertain. Would she listen? 'Will you hear me out?'

She sighed, flopped back into the chair. 'Very well. I'm not going to get any peace until this sorry affair is closed.'

He tilted his head. 'You already know my father left us behind at *Wellington Grange* when he went to England.'

'You mean that's true?' she mocked, stony-faced.

'Yes,' he said quietly, refusing to be unsettled. 'And so is the rest of the story about my mother and sister who live in the States.'

'For goodness' sake, it's your so-called father I'm interested in. If you're his son, why is your name Lewis? Old Tom was known as Lawson?'

'I can only guess. Maybe a business deal went sour? I couldn't ask because I didn't see the old man again after he left for England. We even went to London and tried to make contact with him, but he didn't respond or offer financial help.'

The bitter memories flooded back. 'He literally abandoned us. My mother once told me he was a hard-headed, ambitious man who'd walk over anyone who got in his way. We apparently got in his way.'

'That's not the sweet old man I knew.' She spoke with a sharp-edged tone. 'He was kind, and he loved the garden. Anyone who loves flowers has to be kind and decent.'

'Liz, I'm not going to argue with you,' he growled, shifting uneasily on his feet. 'All I know about him happened more than twenty-five years ago. He must have changed, but why? One thing nobody can dispute — he abandoned his young family and died a wealthy man.'

Her mocking tone knifed into him. 'And that's why you turned up so suddenly. If you haven't been in touch all these years, I'd be interested to hear how you found out he'd died and left a large estate?'

He raised his shoulders. 'I can understand your cynicism, but the fact is I heard he'd returned to Australia and when I came out here to expand my business I decided to try to find him. Perhaps idealistically, I thought we might find some common ground and because of his age, I had to do it now or I might never get another chance. If it turned out he was still an uncompromising, domineering old guy who didn't want to know me, I'd have lost nothing. But I know from what you tell me, he'd reformed.'

Regardless of the implications of his revelation, and the hurt Liz felt, his story drew her in. She leaned forward in to the chair. 'Did you locate him?'

'Not until it was too late. I kept drawing blanks, probably because he'd changed his name, and then I remembered *The Grange* and on a hunch checked it out.

'A neighbour told me an old man lived there and had been taken to the hospital, gravely ill. As his age and appearance vaguely fitted Dad's I decided to follow it up and visit the hospital. 'You may remember you saw me there one morning?'

'I thought you were there on business.' She eyed him suspiciously. 'Tom had died by then.'

'Exactly right, I was there on business that morning. I wanted to donate to the hospital because they'd been so caring to him. I'd visited my dad several times while he was alive. Originally I doubted he was my father — he looked so old, so down-at-heel. I thought he'd fallen on hard times, and he was too ill to recognise me.

'Afterwards, I planned to pay for a private funeral and his hospital bills because the poor old boy seemed destitute. The only signs that anyone visited were lovely flowers by his bed. The nurses told me they were from the florist shop, but I didn't think about it any more.'

'They were from me.'

'Later I guessed as much. Anyway, the hospital told me his lawyer settled his bills with them. Until then I had no idea he actually owned *The Grange* and a large estate.'

'Oh, come on, Steve, the hospital records would have told you it was his address.'

He sighed, discouraged by his failure to convince her he was telling the truth. 'I thought he was the gardener or the caretaker. You said yourself you didn't know he owned the property.'

She laced her fingers in her lap. 'Well, no. I thought he was the caretaker or something like that.'

'Anything else you're not convinced about? Just say and I'll explain.'

'There are a lot of things I'm not convinced about,' she said with spirit.

'For example?'

'How did you find out Tom was the owner?'

'From the hospital records. How did you?' he snapped.

'When I was summoned to the

lawyers' office and told about the will. So where did your information that he'd left everything to me come from?'

'I've already explained that. The estate agency gave me the first lead. I can see why you're doubtful, but when I called on you that first night posing as a journalist, I had followed you from *The Grange*, and knew instinctively you were the one.'

Liz blushed, unsure what he meant, uncertain what to do or say next. The pieces of his story were falling into place. Dare she stop this inquisition and listen to her heart, or push on and rid herself of any doubts, clear up everything standing in her way?

Her head won. 'If you could prove you were Tom's son, why didn't you come straight out and tell me you planned to challenge the will? I'd have respected your honesty, accepted that your family, particularly your mother, had a genuine claim to the estate.'

'It wasn't that I wanted the money, although heaven knows it felt like Tom had thumbed his nose at my mother again. Financially I can take care of her. What I needed was to reassure myself that the old boy hadn't been duped by a fortune-hunting beauty. That may seem odd to you, but he was, after all, my father.'

'And you're sure now?' she said. 'I was never after Tom's money.'

'Yes. Absolutely. I'm convinced you didn't know there was any money. You're a lovely, thoughtful young woman and I . . . '

How she wanted to believe him, but the words 'fortune-hunting beauty' stung. Until she knew, really knew, why his father chose to leave her his estate, she could never put behind her the entrenched idea he still had doubts about her. It was time to walk away.

'Good. Then I can go with a clear conscience. The estate will be transferred across to you. Hayden is already working on it.' She stood up, found his gaze sweeping over her. It was enough to eat into her show of coolness, to unsettle her attempts to stay focused on his story and not on him. Hastily she lowered her eyes and straightened her short skirt around her thighs.

'Liz,' he asked, 'do you think we could be friends again, or have I lost your trust?'

Friends, she questioned herself. Isn't that exactly what Hayden had asked her recently? To his question she'd answered yes, but wasn't it something more enduring she had hoped from Steve?

'How could we be friends while the huge problem of the will remains unresolved? Besides, any relationship we've had only existed because you kept lying . . .'

'That's unfair. The only time I lied was when I posed as a journalist. I didn't know you then, but once I'd met you I knew you were someone special. It's probably not the right time to say this, but I started falling in love with you that next morning when I saw you in the florist shop.'

He moved across to her. Though her heart lurched at his declaration, she dare not give it any weight. Stepping aside, she said quietly, 'Steve, our relationship, if one existed at all, was based on misinformation, and your failure to trust me. You've never been truly open and honest with me. I've had to find out everything by default.'

He dashed his hand through his hair — in a gesture of frustration, she thought. 'Hang it all, Liz. I was hoping you'd understand my dilemma. I didn't want the money or the house, that wasn't my goal in seeking you out. But if you had turned out to be a scheming woman who tricked my old man into leaving you his estate, then I'd planned to fight for it for my mother. Surely you understand. I had to know.'

She strolled across to the other side of the room, turned her back on him. 'And now you know I'm not. Are you quite sure?' she asked in a shaky voice.

'Quite sure. You'd never cheat anyone.' He raised his shoulders, displayed his arms. 'What more can I say?'

'Try goodbye. You can expect to hear from Hayden in a week or two.'

She swung around to leave. He hurried to her side, turned her to face him. His dark blue eyes burned into hers. 'Liz, why can't I convince you the money's not important. I love you.'

He folded her to him as his lips covered her mouth, and for an instant, a brief instant, she surrendered to his kiss. But, too soon, her stomach began to churn. If she wasn't very careful she'd fall under his spell again and trade off all the uncertainties that stood in their way for a few passionate moments in his arms. She forced herself from his hold.

'I can't forget about the money, and if you're truthful, neither can you. While I believed old Tom had no family or friends, I could rationalise his decision to name me in his will. It wasn't easy, but I did it. Now I can't.'

'What you mean is you don't believe

me, you can't forgive me. I've destroyed any chance I had with you.'

As she approached the door, he said bitterly, 'Leaving doesn't resolve anything. I think you're in love with me, too.' His voice softened, 'Bringing us together was the best thing my father has ever done for me, and you're going to spurn that gift? I won't let you.'

Her heart ached, but gripping the handle she forced out the answer her head dictated. 'I'm sorry, but I don't see it that way. If it weren't for his will we might have met somewhere and had a chance. As it is, too much has gone wrong for us, we have too many doubts about one another to have any hope together.'

As she stepped into the hallway, he raised his voice. 'I don't give a blast why Tom left you the money. In fact, I can understand it in a way. I'm crazy about you. I want to marry you.'

Rocketing the door shut behind her, and blinded by tears, she stumbled through the house, out into the cold air and the shelter of her parked car. Their relationship was over before it had even truly begun.

Sharing a take-out Chinese meal, Liz told Angie everything that had happened that day.

'Thanks for listening. I feel better already. You're such a good tonic,' she said afterwards, though her laugh had a phoney tone to it.

'Where to for you and Steve now?'

Liz tried to sound unaffected as she shrugged. 'Nowhere. It was never going anywhere. He didn't trust me, I doubted him. My mother told me not to be blinded by romantic love, and forget the other ingredients for a happy marriage. I think she was right.'

'But he explained everything. You can't blame him for being suspicious in the beginning. He wasn't the only one, I'm sure.'

'You see, Angie, that's the big stumbling block. I've been judged unfairly. The will has brought me nothing but grief.'

'But why don't you believe his story? I think he's deeply in love with you, and by walking away you're making a big mistake. Give him a chance.'

'There was a connection between us. I've never felt that with anyone else, and when he kissed me . . . I . . . '

'You got goosebumps.'

'Grown-ups don't get goosebumps.'

Angie laughed. 'You know what I mean.'

Liz thought for a moment. 'At least now I know I was wasting Hayden's time. That relationship was never going anywhere, either.'

'It's such a shame. You won't believe this, but I've discovered under our legal eagle's self-important exterior lurks a man with an infective sense of humour.'

'Angie, he's learned that from you.' Liz worked up a smile. 'I'm sure you're good for him.'

'I hope so,' she said, 'because I like him. Will you have to see Steve again, or can Hayden handle it all?'

'I'm hoping Hayden can deal with it.

Heaven help me I want to see him, but it's a bad idea. No, it's over.' She forked up some fried rice in thought. So why did her heart still beat for Steve?

'You're determined to sign away all that lovely money. Are you quite sure?'

'Quite, but knowing Hayden, he'll want to play hard ball, force the Lewis family to court to fight for it, but anyone with a conscience could see old Tom's wife should have it. She raised Steve and his sister alone all those years without a penny of support from Tom. So why did that man turn into sweet old Tom and leave me his money? If only I knew.'

Angie's eyes gleamed with mischief. 'He hated his wife, wanted to get back at her for betraying him? Maybe Steve or his sister weren't fathered by him.'

'Oh, sure, but that doesn't explain why he didn't leave everything to the *Lost Dogs' Home*, or the *Save The Children Fund* or even the hospital? There are so many worthy causes. And why change his name?'

'Ah,' Angie grinned, 'some deep dark secret. Maybe he'd been a gangster or guilty of corporate fraud?'

Liz sighed. 'If only there was a credible explanation, one I could accept. I suppose it's understandable that Steve believed I twisted the old man's arm, cast some kind of magic over his father, but it stuck in my brain that deep down he'll never be able to rid himself of the suspicion that I set out to cheat his father.'

'He said he loves you. Why can't you settle for that? Steve and you were meant to be together. Forget all the baggage and get on with it. Accept old Tom's lawyer's explanation, Steve obviously has. He did it because he was fond of you, and very grateful for the time you spent with him.'

Liz stretched. 'I've done all the thinking I can for one day. I'm tired, but I probably won't sleep so let's turn on the telly to see if we can't absorb ourselves in something more exciting than Steve Lewis.'

Her heart leapt as she spoke of his name, for she knew there was nothing, no-one who could excite her more. Not quite trusting him had cost her dearly. Tired and spent, a return to the peaceful, happy and contented life she'd had before he knocked on her door now appealed. She searched for something positive in the last few weeks but could find nothing.

'A murder mystery might do it.' From someone out there she heard Angie suggest as the phone rang. Angie picked it up and handed it to Liz. 'It's Hayden. He's got news for you,' she said seriously.

Liz took it with shaky hands as her thoughts raced back to this afternoon when she'd said her last goodbye to Steve. She took a deep breath, willing it wasn't bad news concerning him. 'What is it, Hayden?' she asked.

Hayden enquired about her health in his usual polite way. Get on with it, she thought, as she said shortly, 'You don't want to know. Why are you calling? The sooner you tell me the quicker I can deal with it.'

'I'm not sure if it's good or bad news, but there's no need to worry, Elizabeth, I can deal with it after we've discussed it. I'd like to come over.'

Frustrated, she sighed loudly. 'Not tonight. I'm trying to forget my day from hell. Tell me why you rang and let me judge if it's good or bad news. We can talk about it tomorrow.'

'Steve Lewis called me at home a short while ago. He informed me his family has no intention of contesting the will. Do you still want to sign it over to them?'

8

Steve tried again. 'Pick up the phone, Liz. Talk to me. Pick it up, please,' he begged allowing frustration to creep into his voice. But it rang on and on. She hadn't answered her phone at home or her mobile in days and he couldn't concentrate on anything until he convinced her his life was nothing without her. She was in his mind, day and night. He had so much he wanted to say to her, to ask her.

He thought often of waiting outside *Fantastic Flowers* or her apartment building until she came out, but she'd probably brush him off without a word.

He would have to think of some other way to contact her, to tell her he loved her, wanted to marry her, didn't think even for a minute she was anything but the kind and sympathetic person his father believed her to be.

It hadn't taken him long to know that, but the wretched will stood between them like a latter day Berlin Wall, keeping them apart. If only he'd been able to reassure her that it didn't matter a tad to him. But in an odd kind of way he understood her sensitivity.

Someone with her natural warmth and loving nature, her honesty, would hate being thought a gold digger. How could he make it up to her, reassure her of the depth of his love.

He sought Angie's advice. She was convinced Liz loved him. Together they arranged for him to call next evening. Angie would invite him in and then go out, leaving them together. It was sneaky, but he wanted her as he had wanted no-one else in his life, and if that's what it took. He lay on his bed, gazing at the ceiling into the early hours of the morning searching for the right words to say when they met.

★ ★ ★

Liz was making up an order for a sheaf of winter lilies when her boss, Melba, came into the workroom.

'That nice young man of yours is asking for you,' she announced.

Liz let out a long irritated breath. Why wouldn't everyone leave her alone? Dropping the flowers on to the bench she hurried across to Melba and whispered harshly, 'He's not my young man and I don't want to see him.'

'I thought you'd been going out with him for some months. I hope you haven't had a parting of the ways. I was expecting you to come in any day with a diamond ring on your finger.' She smiled. 'He's such a gentleman.'

Liz's irritation eased. 'Oh, you mean Hayden?'

'Of course. He's the only young man you're seeing, isn't he?'

Liz shrugged. 'I suppose so.' And strolled into the shop to find Hayden, his back turned to her, admiring the window display.

He swung around at the sound of her

footsteps. 'Lovely,' he said, and crossed to place his lips to her cheek. 'Elizabeth, I meant the flowers, but they're not in your class. I hope you don't mind me calling in?'

'It really isn't a good time.'

He glanced at his watch. 'It's almost one o'clock. I was hoping you could get off for lunch?'

Melba intervened. 'Take all the time you need, Liz. Mondays are usually pretty slow. I can cope.'

It left Liz in an awkward position. She really didn't want to go, she'd rather engross herself in the flowers around her and use her fingers and her mind to create lovely arrangements to cheer other people up. It left her no time to think.

That was the therapy she most needed to shut out the unwelcome dramas of the past few weeks. But because a customer lingered in the shop, obviously listening to the conversation, she forced herself to be gracious and accepted his invitation.

They chose a small coffee shop across the road from the hospital and Hayden ordered sandwiches and coffee before settling beside her at a small round table.

'What was so urgent that you had to interrupt my work?' she asked as he sat down. 'I had planned to ring and make an appointment to see you later today.'

He smiled. 'You don't need an appointment to see me. You know I'll always be here for you.'

She cut him off, wished he would stop being so nice, wished he'd been the one she fell in love with. 'Please, I'm tired of everything associated with the legacy.'

He covered her hand as it rested on the table. 'I can see it hurts, but we have to talk about Steve Lewis, Elizabeth. I'm your legal advisor and it's my duty to inform you of the facts I've discovered about his family. Your friend, old Tom, was formerly Tom Lewis, but that in no way invalidates his will.'

She took a thoughtful bite into her sandwich. 'Steve didn't lie about that?'

'No. Nor did he lie about being the old man's son or that he and his sister were born in Australia and his mother and sister now live in the USA. He's a successful architect in the United Kingdom and recently bought a property to start up a business here. It all checks out.'

'Your point?' she asked.

'As a lawyer, I flatter myself I'm good at judging a man's character, and as much as I hate to admit it, I was wrong about Lewis. After talking to him a couple of times, I'm convinced his objective was never the money.'

She tried to shrug off Hayden's defence. 'Whatever, I can't have Tom's family or anyone else for that matter thinking I schemed and wheedled my way into inheriting his estate.'

'Steve accused you of that?' he demanded.

She clipped hair back from her hot face. 'Not exactly, but I know he thought it. He told me he made contact with me in the beginning to satisfy himself I wasn't an opportunist on the take. It's obscene.'

'Liz, don't distress yourself. Now that he knows you, he certainly doesn't think that. He agrees his father's will is legitimate, and he's adamant he doesn't want the money.'

'Nor do I. I don't know what I was thinking of to have got excited about my good fortune. Good fortune, huh! People were always going to think I duped my way into Tom's life for the money. Own up, didn't you secretly think along those lines yourself?' she spat out.

'Certainly not. Anyone who really knows you would never think that of you. In Lewis' favour, he didn't know you in the beginning.'

'Thank you, Hayden,' she said quietly.

'For what?'

'You don't like the man, but you're big enough to make excuses for him.'

'I was wrong. He's a decent sort. Have you thought of giving him another chance? It's obvious you're miserable without him. He's the same. As I told you earlier I've seen the way he looks at you.'

Her heart tilted. She yearned to say yes, yes, I want to go to him, but there was only one reply she could give.

'Not while I'm living with this ugly thought hanging over my head. Once I reject the legacy nobody can point the finger at me.'

'But you can't put what other people think ahead of your feelings, Liz.'

'To be honest, I regret the day I heard about the will. It's brought nothing but confusion and regrets. My decision to sign over the property to the Lewis family is not negotiable, Hayden. You can be a very persuasive man, but on this you won't win. I don't want *The Grange* or the money, full stop.'

He folded his serviette, said with a touch of disappointment. 'I understand that, but aren't you being a little pig-headed about Lewis? He's the man for you. You're in love with him. Go to him. Sort it out.'

Tears prickled the back of her eyes. 'I want to, but . . . ' she began. The words chocked in her throat.

'Give him a chance to tell you how he feels about you.'

Hayden's advice surprised her. But she judged it as given out of concern for her, and felt some of the ice around her heart begin to melt. She'd been obstinate, put her self-respect before everything else.

'Steve suggested we learn to live with not knowing why Tom named me in the will, but it's a hard ask. I've refused all his attempts to get in touch.'

'He's a smart operator. He truly loves you. He'll find a way.'

'You think so,' she said already feeling a tad easier.

'Call him. Don't wait too long.'

'I'll think about it, but I won't change my mind about refusing the legacy. It cannot remain between us.'

* * *

Restless, Liz, took the stairs to her apartment two at a time. What was the best way to make contact with Steve? Phone? A last visit to *The Grange*?

Angie greeted her at the door. 'There's a letter from Bowlen & Bowlen for you. It was couriered here around four so it must be urgent.'

She had other things on her mind. 'Please, no more surprises today. I'll open it later,' she said. 'I had lunch with Hayden today.'

'Poor Hayden, he's upset. He still doesn't believe you'd dumped him.'

'I didn't dump him, Angie. It was a mutual agreement. Besides, he's urged me to get in touch with Steve.'

'He's given up on you?'

'Yes. He's got his eye on someone else,' Liz said, her mouth curving mischievously.

'And I'm missing out again,' she groaned. 'I've really got to like having that guy around. I understand where he's coming from, and he's got many good qualities.'

Liz nodded. 'I agree with you. I'm still trying to compute it, but he's almost convinced me to talk to Steve. He's sure Steve's in love with me.'

'Huh!' Angie exclaimed, 'I knew that ages ago. You really have had a buttoned-down mind where Mr Lewis is concerned. Forget what your mother taught you, forget what other people may or may not think about you. For goodness sake, chase your dream, Liz. He's right for you.'

With smiling eyes, Angie handed the letter to Liz. 'Now, you'd better read this. Someone else may have left you a legacy.'

Liz tried to grin as she slid her finger under the seal and opened it. A second envelope with her name penned upon it slipped out, and an accompanying letter on the legal firm's letterhead began,

Dear Ms Shepherd, The late Mr Thomas Arthur Lawson wrote the

enclosed letter on the same day he made his will in your favour. He instructed that it be handed to you on the day you were informed of his legacy, and assured us it was a personal note with no legal implications. The letter went on to apologise for its late delivery, due, they claimed, to a change in clerical staff.

'Sounds intriguing.' Angie looked over her shoulder. 'Open it. I can't want to hear what it says?'

Liz shrugged as she examined old Tom's spidery handwriting. 'It's probably a thank-you note.'

For some reason she felt a little shaky as she unfolded the letter and read through the contents, her heart rate increasing as she did.

'Come on, Liz, read it out,' Angie urged her.

⋆ ⋆ ⋆

The following day, excited and restless, she tried to decide the right time and place to contact Steve, but the shop was too busy for her to steal a few moments. Impatience overtook her and she slipped out to the coffee shop and tapped in his number. The answering machine invited her to leave a message. Hang it, why not. 'Steve, I'm in love with you. Call me.'

Although she received no response from him, she felt upbeat at having put all her doubts behind her. After work she arranged a box of chrysanthemums and getting into a warm wool coat, she tossed a colourful scarf around her neck and took a tram to the Melbourne Cemetery. There she enquired about the location of old Tom's grave.

The walk along the rows and rows of headstones seemed endless, depressing. She was about to retrace her steps when around the corner she knew she'd arrived at the right place.

Ahead of her a man bent over the still uncovered earth, rearranging a large floral tribute. His name caught in her throat. She began to run towards him.

He looked up, waved and came to meet her.

'Liz, it's good to see you,' he said casually, though he sounded eager, 'and here we are. Didn't I once suggest to you that my dad found a way to bring us together? He's done it again. It's the only redeeming thought I have about the man I knew as tough, ambitious and ruthless.'

'Who turned into a sweet old guy with a generous heart. Steve,' she said happily, 'I understand everything now. Bowlen & Bowlen sent me a letter from your dad. It explains everything. In it he said he'd lived most of his life as a cheat and a liar who had no compunction about knifing people in the back. That was the man you knew.'

Steve wiped his brow, 'Yeah? He confessed to it? The sly old devil. I'm looking forward to hearing the rest of his letter. Perhaps we'd better find a bench somewhere.'

As Liz read from the letter, Steve followed it, nodding, commenting, occasionally smiling.

Your father and I were in partnership — he the inventor of a piece of farming equipment which sold world-wide, me the business manager. I took out the patent and left for London, cheating your father of his rightful share in the wealth it brought.

Liz grinned, handed him the letter to read. 'So we know everything. Tom grew older, richer, unhappier and friendless. The only way he could find peace in his old age was to return the money to the daughter of the partner he'd cheated. The rest speaks for itself.

'He sought me out, befriended me and made me his sole beneficiary. He always intended for me to know. Poor old darling.'

'Sweetheart, it's the breakthrough you wanted so desperately, but you can't feel sorry for him. He cheated your father, turned him into a morose, moody man, when he'd obviously been a clever, creative person. And left your family battling when they should have been wealthy.'

She looked up at him, her eyes shining. 'But he confessed and tried to make up for his error. If only we'd known earlier, we'd have understood from the start. I should never have doubted you.'

He laughed. 'I hope Hayden doesn't suggest suing the lawyers. Come here.' He reached out to her and took her into his arms. 'My sweet, forgiving Liz,' he whispered against her hair, 'Tom brought us together. I'll always be grateful to him for that.'

Was she mesmerised, or did his smile light up that grey, gloomy afternoon. Did the sunshine creep from behind the clouds and settle in his dark blue eyes?

He placed his arm on hers, faced her, the suggestion of a grin on his lips. 'Not quite.' Then his dark eyes clouded. 'Why didn't you answer my messages?'

'I did — this afternoon. Didn't you get it?'

'No. I've been out all day.'

'You don't know that I'm in love with you?'

His hands cupped her face. He searched deep into her eyes. 'I didn't give up hoping, but it's taken you a long time to admit it.'

She met his searching gaze. 'I let my pride get in the way. I worried that everyone including you thought I was a gold digger.'

'There's nothing standing between us any more.'

A smile touched her lips. 'Nothing.'

'You'd trust me with your life?'

'With my life?' She lowered her voice. 'Is that a marriage proposal?'

'Yes.'

He took her into his arms, kissed her throat, whispered into her hair, 'Will you share the rest of your life with me?'

'Steve, forever and a day. I'm so happy I can't believe it.' A single tear escaped to slide slowly down her cheek. He kissed it away, he cupped her adorable face with his hands. 'A hug might help. And a kiss would seal it.'

His mouth closed over hers and as she surrendered to him she thought that if this was what falling in love felt like, she wanted it to last forever.

The official opening of the house refurbished by the Heart Foundation took place six months after Liz and Steve married.

'It's a beautiful old home. Weren't you vaguely interested in living in it, Liz?' Hayden asked.

Angie, who held his hand, looked up at him and laughed. 'You never really understood Liz, did you? She and Steve were always going to be happy with something small and comfortable. They're not like us. If you've got it, flaunt it is our motto.'

'You mean money, I suppose?' Steve said with a grin.

'She means everything.' Hayden had a glint in his eye. 'This woman has absolutely no inhibitions.'

'And you, Hayden, love the freedom she's given you to be yourself.'

They laughed before Steve said,

kissing his wife, 'The formalities are over. Let's sneak off to our small and comfortable little house before anyone notices.'

'You forgot to mention the lovely garden,' Liz added, with an inviting smile. 'You brought the sunshine into my life, but I couldn't live without flowers either.'

Other titles in the
Linford Romance Library:

A STRANGER'S KISS

Rosemary A. Smith

May, 1849. Sara Osborne has received a strange plea for help from her friend Amelia in Cornwall. Concerned, she travels to the imposing cliff-top house of Ravensmount. There, she meets Tobias Tremaine — whom Sara believed to be Amelia's husband. But Tobias claims they never married — and Amelia is missing . . . The mystery deepens as Sara meets Tobias's strange siblings and their father, Abraham. But how does the enigmatic Tamsin fit into the family? What is the secret of Amelia's music box? And will Sara succumb to a stranger's kiss?

RIVALS IN LOVE

Toni Anders

Bryony becomes private secretary to Justin, a charismatic but moody novelist. She finds him attractive — until she meets Rowan, his charming cousin. The two men have been estranged for years since they and Eleanor, whom they both loved, were caught up in a tragedy. Bryony risks Justin's wrath in her attempts to bring about a reconciliation between the cousins. But then she faces a dilemma — which man does she really love? And will history repeat itself?

WINTERHAVEN

Janet Whitehead

Annabel Tyler's boss sent her to the Scottish Highlands to save Winterhaven, the estate of a valued client. But at every turn Annie found a mystery to unravel. Who was David O'Neal, the stranger who seemed to know all about her? What was the dark secret of Winterhaven's deep loch? And were the estate and its inhabitants cursed? But then Annie fell in love with the new master of Winterhaven — and things took an even more dramatic turn!

UNBREAK MY HEART

Beth James

Despite her broken heart, artist Roberta Armstrong has put everything into rebuilding her business and her life. Whilst her friend Lee wants to take their friendship further, she is determined not to let anyone become close to her again. Then Charles arrives . . . Slowly her heart begins to mend, and she truly feels she can put her tragic past behind her. But is Charles hiding something? And will Bobbie ever be able to learn to trust again?

SAVE YOU

Beverley

Donna McGuire is
ranch she inherite
grandfather. But s
in the community,
any credit. Someone is sabotaging
her business. Could it be her
grandfather's trusted friend, the
handsome Jared Jackson, who has
made no secret of the fact that he
finds her incompetent and wants her
land? And what is she to do about
Amy-Kate, Jared's small daughter,
who is determinedly looking for a
new Mamma